A CLIMATE OF DOUBT

Russell F. Moran

A Climate of Doubt
Coddington Press
Copyright © 2018 by Russell F. Moran
Printed in the United States of America
ISBN (print) - 13: 978-0-9990003-6-6

www.morancom.com

DEDICATION

This book is dedicated to the emergency first responders of the world.

ACKNOWLEDGEMENTS

As always, I thank my wife, Lynda, for her attentive reading and rereading of my many drafts, and for laughing at my jokes. I also thank my friend and copy editor, John White, for his proofreading and editing. And I especially thank my readers, many of whom are a constant source of inspiration and encouragement for me.

AUTHOR'S NOTE

You will find a **Cast of Characters** after the last chapter of the book. It can be frustrating to come across a character on page 150, who you first met on page 20, especially if you've put the book down for a few days. I've seen this done in Russian literature, and I happily add a cast of characters to *A Climate of Doubt* as well as my other novels.

CHAPTER ONE

July 16

It was gradual, almost imperceptible, creeping up on us like an animal. We didn't think about it at first; then, we couldn't think about anything else.

"My God, it's cold," Ellen yelled.

"Cold? A few minutes ago it was 98 degrees. We're in a heat wave, remember?"

"Rick, look at me. Forget what you heard before on the radio. Tell me how you *feel*."

"I'm freezing my ass off, but that's impossible. It's July 16th."

"Maybe it's impossible, but let's get into the house and talk about it over hot chocolate."

Ellen and I were staying at our beach house in East Hampton.

"Steve, we're heading inside," I said into my phone. "I don't know what the hell is going on with this weather, but no sense all of us freezing our butts off. We can find out more information on the TV." Steve Trent is the head of my Secret Service detail.

We were only a couple of hundred feet from the house. The temperature dropped with each step we took. Just moments before, we were walking along the beach, cooling ourselves from the blistering heat wave.

I shook my head to adjust to our suddenly crazy reality. It was freezing cold—on July 16. Steve Trent walked to the back of the great room and looked out at the thermometer on the porch.

"It's 35 degrees, Rick," he said. "A few minutes ago, it was 98. That's a 63-degree drop in about five minutes."

I walked over to the thermostat, clicked off the air conditioning, and turned on the heat. It's electric heat—expensive as hell but fast and efficient. Our house is huge, especially for only two people, but we entertain out-of-town guests and relatives a lot. The house is 5,000 square feet, covering two stories and surrounded by decks and walkways. The siding is cedar shake, in keeping with Hamptons-style architecture. Two years ago, the house won first prize for country homes by *Architectural Digest*, which wasn't surprising because Ellen, my multi-talented wife, designed it. Ellen's a partner in the Manhattan architectural firm of Whitney, Cox, and Bellamy. She's also a brand-new TV star, which results in a ton of money.

I married well.

Steve's guys were speaking into their shirt lapels, a second nature way of communicating for a Secret Service agent. They looked like they were performing an improv comedy routine. As Secretary of Homeland Security, I'm assigned a team of five Secret Service agents.

Ellen reached under the staircase and dragged out a large trunk. She opened the top and tossed me a pair of jeans, a sweatshirt, and a woolen sweater. She also took out a bunch of blankets, sweaters, and sweat suits for the Secret Service guys.

I wrapped a blanket around Ellen's shoulders as I turned to Steve Trent and the other agents.

"If anybody has any idea what the hell is going on with this weather, don't be shy, speak up."

I looked out at the wall thermometer on the porch. It was now 29 degrees outside.

CHAPTER TWO

"Good afternoon, ladies and gentlemen, Wolf Blitzer here for CNN. It's been a long time since I worked as a weatherman, but today's weather *is* the news, the big news, almost the only news. Today is July 16, and those of us in the East woke up this morning to the second week of a scorching heat wave, with temperatures in the upper 90s for 10 days in a row. Well, the heat wave broke today, in a way nobody could have predicted. The current temperature in Central Park is 27 degrees. Across the nation, thermometers dropped over 60 degrees in less than an hour. The numbers are similar, not only across the country but across the world. Tomorrow's headlines will all be a variation of 'Cold Wave Grips the Earth in Mid-July.' Before we try to analyze the situation, I want to help our viewers cope with the problem. Later we'll attempt to figure it out.

"Freezing pipes are a menace in conditions like this, and a burst pipe in your home can make your life miserable. It can be dangerous as well. I want to remind you, if you need reminding, to ignore the calendar and get dressed for winter."

The phone rang, and Ellen put the TV on pause. It was President Blake. "Tell me what you know about this insane weather, Rick."

"As of right now, Mr. President, I don't know more than anyone else. I'm about to call the State and Defense Departments to see what's going on with them."

"My guess is that your wife Ellen and her army of news people are putting together a special program for *The Ellen Bellamy Show* as we speak. Sometimes TV people are miles ahead of the government when tracking unfolding emergencies."

"Yes, Ellen's on the case, Mr. President, and she's feeding me information as she gets it from the news desk at NBC. We were walking along the beach when the freeze hit. The thermometer just dropped another few degrees. It's 23 degrees in East Hampton. I'll call you as soon as I find out anything, sir."

As soon as I find out anything? What the hell is there to find out when the temperature drops over 60 degrees in minutes? One thing I did know— our world had just turned upside down, and we were in serious trouble.

CHAPTER THREE

John Jay Park on the FDR Drive and 78th Street in Manhattan is a popular destination for New Yorkers on hot summer days. July 16, a scorching hot Sunday, saw a capacity crowd at both of its pools. The intermediate pool is big—145 by 45 feet, and was packed with splashing children. Older kids and adults used the nearby diving pool.

Myrna Jackson sat on a bench with her sister Jane Bauman as they watched Myrna's six boys in the pool.

"I don't care if this pool is for kids," Myrna said, "I'm going in. It's too goddam hot sitting on this bench."

She walked down the wide steps to enter the pool.

"What the hell is going on?" she yelled, holding her arms and shivering.

Tom Barton, a lifeguard, sat next to his friend and lifesaving partner Dianne Puleo. His body tensed as the freezing wind blew across the pool. He stood, blew his whistle, and shouted into his megaphone.

"Everybody out of the water," he yelled. "Get inside the building— *NOW.*"

As the kids climbed out of the pool the sudden freeze came on them in a claw-like grip. The sound of 95 screaming children added to the bizarre reality of a freezing wind in mid-summer. Barton and Puleo ran to the entrance of the indoor facility and waved the kids and parents inside.

"I hope this building is heated," a woman yelled as she dragged her five-year-old to the entrance.

"This park closes after Labor Day, ma'am," Barton said. "There's no heat, but at least you'll be out of the wind."

He looked at the thermometer on the outside wall, which read 23 degrees. The wind picked up and was blowing at 30 mph.

"Get the hell inside, Tom," Dianne shouted.

"No. I'm staying right here until everybody is in the building."

"Do you have anything warm to put on?"

"Just the tee shirt and bathing suit that you're looking at."

She tossed him a beach towel.

After standing for 20 minutes in the freezing wind, Barton was satisfied that everyone was inside.

When he walked in his eyes blurred and he felt dizzy. He grabbed the edge of a table to steady himself, and then collapsed to the floor, unconscious.

Two weeks later, Tom Barton would die at Lenox Hill Hospital from complications of hypothermia.

***

"We couldn't have picked a better day for a regatta," Tony Ulewicz said to his wife Margie. Tony was the commodore of the South Bay Cruising Club, an organization of sailing enthusiasts on Long Island's South Shore. Fifteen sailboats competed in the regatta on the Great South Bay. They had just rounded the first buoy and tacked to head southwest, at a sharp angle to the wind.

"I'd like to stay on this tack for the rest of the day," Margie said. "It keeps the wind in our face."

"Hey, what's that? What the hell is going on?"

"God almighty, it's cold," Margie yelled as she wrapped a towel around her shoulders.

Without prompting from anyone, the entire fleet tacked to head north for the marina in Bay Shore.

"Hey, what's wrong with Mike Plimpton?" Margie said, pointing to a boat off to starboard.

Seventy-five-year-old Plimpton, sailing alone, released the tiller and slumped over, holding his chest.

"Shit, it looks like Mike's having a heart attack," Tony said. He turned to aim straight for Plimpton, and then tacked to come alongside. Margie took the tiller as Tony jumped onto Plimpton's boat.

"I think he's dead, Margie. Take our boat in and I'll follow."

The statistics for the regatta weren't what Tony had hoped for. Eight cases of hypothermia, one death from a heart attack, 20 incidents of frostbite, and one nervous breakdown.

***

"Hey Jack, slow down," EMT Patty Carmichael said to Jack Maloney the ambulance driver. "We're coming up on that spot where the tanker truck spilled water this morning."

"Don't worry Patty, it's just water."

They drove along Montauk Highway in West Islip on their way to Good Samaritan Hospital with an accident victim in the back. His siren blaring, Maloney drove as fast as he could.

"It's getting kind of cold in here, Patty. Turn off the air conditioning."

As he rounded a bend in the road, the ambulance hit a patch of black ice and careened out of control. A car behind them clipped their rear end, spinning the ambulance into oncoming traffic. They collided head-on with a cement truck, killing them both, along with the patient in the back and the nurse who attended him.

***

"Ready for a great day of *geezer golf*, Bill?"

Frank Montrose and Bill Fleming had just left the club house and headed for the first tee of the annual Senior Golf Tournament, sponsored by the Great River Golf Club. The outing was restricted to people over age

65. The tournament rules allowed for no golf carts, to encourage cardiovascular exercise, and to mimic the USGA and PGA rules. Each golfer towed his own hand-drawn golf caddy. The location for this year's tournament was the Bellport Country Club, bordering on the Great South Bay of Long Island. The tournament committee had considered cancelling because of the blistering heat, but decided to go forward because there were always cooling breezes from the bay. A refreshment cart circled the tournament with free bottles of ice water and Gatorade.

Frank walked up to the tee on the 15th hole, a par four overlooking the bay. After he birdied the 14th hole, Frank was feeling good, if a bit exhausted from dragging his golf caddy in the 95-degree heat. As he raised his club, his arms dropped involuntarily in response to a sudden freezing wind off the bay.

"What the hell is that all about?" Frank yelled.

"I wish I had an answer, Frank. Let's get our asses into the clubhouse."

The clubhouse was 200 yards from where they stood on the 15th tee. Both men, each age 74, were already exhausted and sweaty from their first 14 holes. When they walked into the clubhouse, Bill sat down on the first available chair. He slumped over, his face ashen white. He would be pronounced dead of a heart attack later that day.

The reception room in the clubhouse was a chaotic scene of confused people, some wrapping themselves in tablecloths to try to get warm. The sounds of emergency vehicle sirens punctuated the sudden end of the golf tournament.

***

"Okay, everybody, line up," Boy Scout Leader Mel Borden yelled. "This is a cleanup day, and you all know what that means. We're going to leave this camp just like we found it—clean and neat. I want three feet between each scout. Walk slowly and pick up any piece of debris you see. It's hot as hell, as you all know, so don't walk too fast. I don't want anybody passing out from a heat stroke."

Mel Borden and the 50 kids of Boy Scout Troop 871 from Greenport, Long Island, were wrapping up their week of camping at Boy Scout Camp

Wooten in the Catskills. The school bus that would take them home was scheduled to arrive at 11 a.m., two hours from then. His younger brother, Mike Borden was the Assistant Scout Leader. Mel, age 50, was doing what he loved— working with kids, something he didn't get to do on his job as a stock broker.

During the week at Camp Wooten, Mel kept running activities to a minimum, something he hated to do, but the 95-degree temperature called for caution.

They finished their cleanup at 10 a.m.

"Okay, guys, everybody into the bunkhouse and grab your duffel bags. We're going to line up right here and wait for the bus."

As the last boy came to the staging area with his bag, all the scouts yelled out with one voice— "Whoa."

"What the hell is going on?" Mel said to his brother Mike. "It's freezing."

Mike walked up the steps to the bunkhouse and looked at the thermometer.

"It's 32 degrees, Mel. A few minutes ago, it was in the 90s."

"Everybody inside. Leave your bags where they are. I don't know what's going on, but I don't want us all to freeze."

The inside temperature was still warm from the heat wave that had just disappeared, but it was starting to cool fast. Outside, it began to snow.

At 11:15 a.m. Mel tried to call Andy Timmons, the school bus driver. He was 15 minutes late.

"I don't have any cell phone reception, Mike. Try yours."

Mike's phone was dead as well.

Twenty minutes before Mel tried to call, Timmons' bus had hit a patch of black ice as he drove around a curve. The bus spun out of control, and tumbled end over end down a steep embankment. Timmons' frozen body was found a week later.

On Tuesday, July 18, an Army National Guard Humvee with a snow plow attached, paved the way for a school bus. They pulled into Camp Wooten. The sergeant in charge of the search walked into the bunkhouse, and almost passed out from shock at what he saw. All 50 scouts, along with Mel and Mike Borden, were lying on the floor. Mel's idea was to take advantage of their bodies' thermal heat. The clubhouse was designed for summer and had no fireplace or other source of heat. Mel's action saved a few lives, but two boys died of hypothermia.

CHAPTER FOUR

My wife, Ellen, was signed by NBC last year to host an afternoon talk show called *The Ellen Bellamy Show*. The show took off and soon became a TV phenomenon, rivaling *Judge Judy*. The money she earns from NBC plus her huge architectural fees resulted in our beautiful beach house, as well as a brownstone in Greenwich Village in downtown Manhattan. My salary as a cabinet secretary, although not bad, would never provide the luxuries we enjoy.

Whenever something big hits the news, you can expect to see total coverage on the most popular talk show on television, *The Ellen Bellamy Show*. A deep freeze in July fit the bill for Monday's show.

***

I was still having a hard time coming to grips with the fact that Ellen and I were walking along the ocean this morning when the sizzling 98 degree temperature suddenly dropped to below freezing. As Secretary of Homeland Security, people expect me to have answers. I didn't. I didn't even know what questions to ask.

"I could get used to this place, Mr. Secretary," Steve Trent said as he and a couple of other agents loaded the bags into our car.

Steve drove, with the other agents in a car behind us. Ellen was working the phone, talking to her producers. I called the Office of Emergency Preparedness, an agency that wasn't prepared for this emergency.

We definitely weren't prepared for what happened next.

CHAPTER FIVE

July 16 - Afternoon

"Mr. President, turn around and look out the window," Chief of Staff Jake Arnold said as he handed the president a cup of coffee.

A blizzard, not just snow flurries, but a full blizzard with blinding snow and driving wind hit without warning. The snow looked even more bizarre because it came down on the lush mid-July greenery of the Rose Garden. The thermometer outside the window read 20 degrees.

"Good afternoon folks," said Ben Stratton, the TV weather reporter for CBS. "I hope you're adjusting to the bizarre cold spell we're having on this July 16th afternoon. Well, I have some more chilling news for you. A warm front is approaching from the west with balmy temperatures around 30 degrees. In weather reporting, a warm front doesn't necessarily mean warm; it means that an approaching front is warmer than the temperature overhead. Often that means moisture and precipitation. In the pattern we're looking at, the result of this warm front is going to be staggering. The National Weather Bureau predicts the worst blizzard in 100 years will hit the D.C. Metropolitan area beginning after 6 p.m. this evening. But if you look out your window, you'll see that it's begun already. Fortunately, it's a Sunday, so traffic should be at a minimum. Authorities across the region are asking people to stay home and whatever you do, don't take your car on the road. Computer models are projecting snowfall reaching five feet in the Capital, with similar totals across the region. And this storm will be no gentle sprinkling of white stuff. Winds are predicted to reach 55 miles per hour across the region."

***

"My taping for tomorrow's show is ready to go as soon as I get there," Ellen said. "The producers are still putting together the guest list, according to a text I just got. I hope to hell they don't book the standard-issue climate-change fanatics. I can picture some clown trying to convince the viewers that he predicted this strange crap."

***

Steve Trent parked our car in the garage under our brownstone and called for a government SUV to take me to my nearby office at 26 Federal Plaza. Since I became Homeland Security Secretary, the government assigned five Secret Service agents to be with me at all times. Sam Thornton, another agent, was waiting for me. Steve Trent then drove Ellen to the NBC studio at Rockefeller Center, the snow having already accumulated to three inches. I called my department heads and told them to keep in touch with the office by their secure phones and Intranet connections. No sense dragging people in when they can stay in touch remotely.

When I got to my office I walked over to the window, not believing what I saw—the snow had become a blizzard.

CHAPTER SIX

July 17

Sarah Watson, Director of the FBI, was at 26 Federal Plaza to prepare for a meeting with me and the head of the Joint Terrorism Task Force, my former position.

Sarah's an old friend, and, as my former boss, we didn't have go through the formalities of getting to know each other. She knocked and walked into my office. I was standing by the window talking on the phone and waved her in. My conversation ended and we both looked out at the strengthening blizzard.

"You and I have been through some weird shit over the years, Rick, but nothing tops this," Watson said as she stared out the window.

"I just got off the phone with the White House," I said. "As a cabinet officer I shouldn't say this, but the president has some real assholes on his staff. One of them just said to me, and get this, 'You've got to do something,' as if I can control the goddam weather."

Sarah laughed.

"I'm happy that I have you between me and the White House," Sarah said.

"Mr. Secretary, your wife, Ellen, is on line one," my assistant said over the intercom.

"Hi, hon, enjoying the view?" I said as I put the phone on speaker. "I'm here with Sarah Watson."

"Hi Sarah," Ellen said. "Both of you will want to catch my show in 10 minutes. I have a special guest who has a wild theory about this weather."

"Please tell me he's not some messianic climate-change nut who wants to blame everything on carbon dioxide," I said.

"I can't guarantee that he's not, but he seems to be a sharp guy. He was on my show last week, if you recall, talking about the heat wave. He knows me well and he knows not to pull some nonsense with me. I gotta get ready. Stay tuned."

"You married a wonderful lady, Rick. I'm glad she's on our side."

CHAPTER SEVEN

July 17

"Welcome to *The Ellen Bellamy Show*. I'm your host, Ellen Bellamy. I like this show so much I even named myself after it."

Sarah looked at me with a pained expression.

"I love that woman, lame jokes and all," I said.

"Today's show is dedicated to our strange weather. To put it mildly, not to pun, we're all experiencing a bout of weather that we never felt before, or even imagined."

Ellen, who's partially at the mercy of her make-up department, wore earmuffs and a big scarf around her neck. The costume was her idea.

"Our guest today is from the NOAA, the National Oceanic and Atmospheric Administration, and he's got some shocking thoughts for us. Before I introduce him, our resident meteorologist, Al Roker, will give us an update on our beautiful July weather."

The camera panned on the familiar face of Al Roker. Al, who is as much a showman as a weatherman, was dressed in a winter coat with a hat and earflaps. He also wore huge woolen mittens.

"Good afternoon, folks, Al Roker here for *NBC Weather*. I usually give you an overview of the national weather and then introduce your local meteorologist to announce the weather 'in your neck of the woods.' But today is different. Your 'neck of the woods' is *our* 'neck of the woods.' The conditions across the entire country, even most parts of the world, are eerily the same—a freezing winter-weather pattern in mid-July. I'm confident that I'm speaking for everyone when I say that we never experienced anything like this. Yesterday morning we were still in the grips of a massive heatwave, with temperatures throughout the area over 90 degrees. Then suddenly, and I mean suddenly, the mercury dropped—like a rock. Within minutes we were shuddering from the cold. Then came a warm front with a ton of moisture, resulting in the blizzard we're experiencing now. As strange as the conditions are in the New York Metropolitan area, it gets even weirder as we look to the south. Here is Lilly Morton with our NBC affiliate in Fort Lauderdale in Southern Florida—that's *Southern* Florida."

Lilly stood on a marina dock wearing arctic gear and bracing her body against the fierce wind and snow.

"Hi, everyone. Lilly Morton here for NBC. The scene behind me tells you all you need to know about today's storm, folks. That huge mound of snow that you're looking at is piled on top of a 75-foot yacht. Here is a photo of the boat when it docked yesterday morning after a cruise."

She showed a blown-up picture of a beautiful yacht with people in bathing suits on deck waving—yesterday morning.

Roker continued his report from various locales across the country and ended up with a shot of the Champs-Elysees in Paris—covered in snow.

"For some in-depth analysis of what the heck is going on we return now to *The Ellen Bellamy Show*, where Ellen has a special guest from NOAA."

The camera panned to Ellen, who had by now ditched her arctic costume.

"Thanks for your usual thorough reporting, Al," Ellen said. "My guest today is Professor Dwight Peterson, a vice president of the board of NOAA, where he has served for over 20 years. He's also chairman of the department of climate studies at Georgetown University. Professor Peterson has some fascinating things to tell us about our weird weather."

Peterson looked every bit the professor that he is, wearing a plaid jacket and monotone shirt. His hair was scrupulously disheveled, his reading glasses perched on the edge of his nose.

"Professor, tell us your thoughts on this amazing weather that's gripped most of the world. Were you as shocked as the rest of us?"

"Yes, Ellen, I was shocked—shocked but not surprised. Let me explain that cryptic remark I just made. First let me say that this incident is typical of climate change. The phenomenon is real, and we're all trying to figure out how it happened. But this event puts an exclamation point on the words climate change."

"I'm surprised to hear you say that, professor. Most people assumed that climate change is a slow-moving process, but let's face it, it sure feels like the climate has changed."

"Climate change *is* a long slow process, Ellen, although it's become more rapid in recent years. Climate change is real, although a lot of people deny it. Something is interfering with our major weather-maker, the sun. Something has changed the way the sun's rays hit earth in a drastic way. That's the way climate change works, and the tons of carbon dioxide that we pump into the atmosphere contributes heavily to it."

"But how could that possibly happen, professor?" Ellen asked with a look of confusion. One of the reasons Ellen's show is so popular is that she has an uncanny ability to let the viewers see real feelings expressed on her face.

"Ellen, I'm not going to shoot my mouth off with unproven theories. I strongly believe that we're seeing the natural result of climate change, although we don't understand yet what's going on."

"There you have it folks, words of wisdom from a climate studies expert. On a typical July 17th I would normally end the show by suggesting that you go home and fire up the barbecue grill, but instead I'll just say, 'bundle up and get home safely.'"

CHAPTER EIGHT

"It's Ellen Bellamy on line two, Director Watson," Sarah's assistant said.

Sarah picked up the phone and put it on speaker.

"I was just about to call *you*," I said. "Sarah and I want to meet this guy Peterson. I'll send an SUV to pick you up."

"He's splitting a gut to talk to you two. He's got a lot more to say than he did on my show. We'll be there in a few minutes."

Sarah Watson and I looked out the window at the still growing blizzard. We could make out a police SUV pulling up onto the sidewalk and driving part-way into the entrance of the building. A minute later the intercom sounded, and Sarah's assistant announced the arrival of Ellen and her special TV guest.

Sarah Watson and Ellen had become good friends over the three years we've been married. She constantly tried to recruit Ellen into the FBI but realized that her gigantic TV salary would be hard to match. I had to agree with Sarah that Ellen would make an excellent FBI agent. Two years ago, Ellen was kidnapped by an ISIS cell and held for ransom at a terrorist safe-house in New Jersey. An FBI SWAT team stormed the building, but it was Ellen's courage and use of an AK-47 that saved the day. Ellen is sweet, pretty, and tough as leather.

Ellen and Peterson walked in after hanging up their winter outfits in the cloakroom. The temperature was 25 degrees, to everyone's constant amazement.

"I know you both saw Professor Peterson on my show this afternoon, but he told me he has some things that he'd like to talk to you about, without it being made public on TV."

Peterson was a friendly guy, in a rumpled professorial sort of way. I wondered if he was as smart as he looked. Sarah got up and brought a tray with coffee which she placed in front of Peterson. She often does things like that to grab somebody's attention. People don't expect the Director of the FBI to serve them coffee.

"Ellen tells us that you would like to discuss something that wasn't part of your statements on TV," I said. "Please let us know what you have in mind. In view of this insane weather, we're open to anything."

"As I said on Ellen's show a short while ago," Peterson said, "I'm shocked but not surprised by this bizarre weather event, and you'll see shortly why I didn't want to go public with these thoughts. I'm of the opinion that not only is this weather a result of climate change, but it's likely to continue."

"At the risk of appearing dense," Watson said, "why do you think it will continue?"

"Director Watson," Peterson said, "I'm thinking this way because this weather hit us with no warning. Hell, meteorology has come a long way in the past few years, especially with satellites to help with long-term predictions. We believed we'd never get blindsided like the people in Galveston, Texas, by a hurricane nobody knew was coming. That was 1900, over a hundred years ago. We thought the days of a sudden weather event hammering us were over, until yesterday morning. Not only did we not see this freezing spell coming, we had no warning of any kind, not even slight. It just slammed into us, followed by this wicked blizzard—in the middle of the summer."

"Dr. Peterson, I have a lot of respect for you," I said. "I've read a few of your articles on climate change and I found them compelling. But I must ask you a blunt question. Do you have any idea how this happened?"

"No, I don't," Peterson said. "I could be dishonest and make up some ideas, but I would rather stick to the facts. The reason I asked to see you and Director Watson is simple—climate change has suddenly gone from an academic subject to a very real phenomenon. I say that based on my knowledge of the climate and of weather patterns. But forget about me and my credentials. All three of you are extremely bright people. Ask yourselves how an event like this could occur out of nowhere, and contrary to everything we know about changing weather. The one innocent party in this mess is Mother Nature. You people investigate and solve problems before they occur, but we're suddenly hit by something that you couldn't foresee."

"So, if I understand you correctly" I said, "this weather may be caused by a sudden acceleration of climate change."

"Yes, I am. I can't see any other possibility."

"Thank you, Dr. Peterson," I said. "I know that you have another appointment uptown at Columbia, so we won't detain you any further. Given the conditions outside, it may take you a while to get there. I can have a government SUV take you there, but you may do better to take the subway. Thank you for coming in. I'm sure I'll be calling on you in the future."

CHAPTER NINE

Ellen, Sarah, and I remained seated after Peterson left. I walked over to the window. It was 6:15 p.m. Hard to believe it was still summer, and sundown wouldn't happen for another couple of hours at 8:23 p.m., making it broad daylight outside. The street looked like a down comforter, perfectly smooth except for slight bumps. Under the bumps were cars, busses, and trucks. The atmosphere is my office was hot and sticky. Understandably, the HVAC system went batshit with the sudden change from heat and humidity to bitter cold. Yesterday the system was calling for cool dry air. Now it demands heat.

"So, what do we think about this guy, Peterson?" I said. "Is he the real deal, and if so should we pay much attention to him? He doesn't have any specific answers, only theories."

"I have a hard time taking this guy seriously," Ellen said. "We're faced with a weird situation and what does he come up with? A bizarre theory that the climate has suddenly changed. But it's a smart move. He knows that the best way to get rebooked on my show, as well as a lot of other talk shows, is to come up with something controversial, something juicy, almost like the script for a TV crime drama. I think that's why he asked to meet with you and Sarah. He wants to build up the suspense. Before we left the set to come here, he made it a point to let me know that he would be in town for a few days, staying at his brother's apartment here in Manhattan. I've seen a lot of academic types like him. Once they get a taste of celebrity status, they want to keep it going. This guy is one sharp operator. Let me suggest this. I'd like to get Al Roker, the NBC meteorologist, on the phone. Al isn't just a TV weatherman who knows how to point to stuff on a weather map. He's studied his field and has become a real meteorologist. He works as a TV weatherman because he couldn't turn down the huge salary we pay him."

"Go for it, hon." I said. "Let's hope he's still there."

"NBC, how may I direct your call?" said the operator.

"Hi Janet, this is Ellen Bellamy. Please put me through to Al Roker if he's still there."

"He's still here, Ellen. Like most of us, he's camping out in the studio tonight."

"Sunshine and flowers Roker here. What's up Ellen?"

"You saw my show with that climate expert professor Peterson, Al. I'm here at FBI Headquarters downtown where Peterson asked to be taken after the show. To get right to the point, Al, this guy Peterson has come up with a theory that this crazy weather event may be caused by a sudden acceleration of climate change. I'm here with my husband, Rick, whom you've met before, and Sarah Watson, Director of the FBI. We'd like your opinion on Peterson's theory that the climate has changed overnight."

"As a plot for a science fiction novel it's a great idea," Roker said, "but the effect of climate change on the immediate weather is minimal. We've tried over the years to change the weather conditions. We've even tried seeding clouds with chemicals to fight droughts, but with little success. My opinion is that the weird weather we find ourselves in is the result of phenomena that we haven't discovered yet. I know that may not be a satisfying answer but it's the truth. We just don't know yet what's caused this crap. Peterson's ideas may be good for exciting television, but as scientific theory

I wouldn't pay attention to it unless he comes forward with some evidence. Hey, I'm due to be on the air with a special additional segment of my show. Because of the circumstances I'll be doing the show live, not taped. Make sure you guys catch it. I'll be breaking some wild new weather news."

"Al, thank you for your input," Ellen said. "I'm sure Rick and Director Watson may want to talk to you further if anything becomes of this."

"Sarah, your thoughts?" I said.

"I'm inclined to agree with Ellen, especially after hearing Al Roker's comments. Peterson was too smooth, and hatched a bunch of ideas out of the air with no evidence whatsoever. I don't think we should allocate a lot of resources based on Peterson's ideas."

"Well, it looks like we have a unanimous opinion about Professor Peterson," I said. "But we shouldn't dismiss him so fast. Sarah, when you were my boss at the FBI, you taught me the value of talking to apparent nut-jobs just to see what they had to say. Maybe we should see more of Peterson on TV talking about his theory. Ellen, would you consider having him back on your show?"

"I'll bet you anything that my producers are already planning another show with Peterson," Ellen said. "I don't get to veto what the producers want, and they want exciting television, as Al Roker put it. Let's catch Al's weather report."

CHAPTER TEN

"Good evening, ladies and gentlemen, Al Roker here. The blizzard continues on this strange day of July 17. Ever since I've been reporting the weather over the years, I always begin my report by announcing any upcoming changes in a current weather pattern. I expected to do that this evening, but I can't. Look at this radar image, and you'll see what I'm talking about. We're stuck in a gigantic snowstorm that shows no signs of ending. That's right, I can't predict when this monster is going to roll over and die. It just keeps pounding us across most of the nation and the world. The only thing I can predict, based on our estimate of three inches an hour, is that we'll see over eight feet of snow by midnight at our reporting station in Central Park. The accumulation for Eastern Long Island, with its additional moisture off the ocean, is even more dramatic. We expect to see 10 feet of snow based on the weather station at Long Island-MacArthur Airport in Islip. History is being made as I speak, and we hope that this history will soon be behind us, but that I can't predict."

Roker walked over to a new graphic.

"Here are some of the shocking accumulation predictions for the next few hours at some of our major reporting stations. The numbers I'm about to give you are for midnight, Eastern Time, about five and a half hours from now:

Hartford, Connecticut – 11 Feet
Boston, Massachusetts – 12 Feet
Newport, Rhode Island – 10 Feet
Newark, New Jersey – 9 Feet
Islip, New York – 10 Feet

The camera panned to the street outside the studio where Janet Bowden, a reporter, stood in the swirling snow. She was dressed for the arctic.

"Hi, everybody, Janet Bowden here for NBC. Underneath this beautiful snow mountain behind me is a Mr. Softee ice cream truck. One of the few positive things about this blizzard is that it we've gotten a break from the mind-numbing jingles the truck plays constantly. An interesting thing about this rapidly accumulating snow is that it's becoming difficult to tell if there's anything under the drifts, although we know that there are countless cars, trucks, and busses under the white stuff."

"Thanks, Janet," Roker said. "The bottom line, folks, is that we will see an accumulation of snow above 10 feet throughout the region. The thing to keep in mind is this—we don't see any end to this storm. Needless to say, the blizzard is creating some dangerous, even life-threatening conditions. I'm cutting now to City Hall, where Mayor Bill Adams is about to make a statement."

CHAPTER ELEVEN

"Good evening, my fellow New Yorkers and our neighbors throughout the Metropolitan Area," Mayor Adams said. "I don't have any book to follow in discussing this storm because we've never seen anything like it before. Some folks have named it the Millennium Blizzard, and I think that's an appropriate title. I know you expect me to urge you to stay off the roads, but this storm presents a new twist. I'm not going to just urge you or warn you because the storm is speaking for itself. You simply can't get anywhere on the roads. Even emergency vehicles are having a hard time getting around. A stalled or snowed-in car makes matters a lot worse. I'm announcing a temporary local law just passed by the City Council making it a Class-E felony to drive a non-emergency vehicle without the express permission from the local Office of Emergency Management. That may sound drastic, but this storm *is* drastic. The number to call is behind me on the screen. Because this storm hit with absolutely no warning, a lot of you were unable to stock up on necessities like food and prescription drugs. Now is the time to be a neighbor in spirit, not just in name. If you have extra food, please share it with someone in need. We had in the works a plan to deliver prescription drugs by aerial drones, but the wind gusts up to 60 mph have made that impossible. If the wind dies down we're going to execute the drone plan. We're going to back that plan up with the National Guard delivering emergency medicine in snow-friendly Humvees. Please contact your doctor and follow instructions if you run out of your medication. Oil heat is another serious challenge for us. Because this storm hit us in mid-July, few people thought of topping off their oil tanks. Please use common sense and conserve fuel as much as possible. Rather than crank up the heat, put on a sweater or wrap yourself in a blanket. Keep water taps turned on to a trickle and keep cabinet doors under sinks open to avoid frozen pipes. We're experiencing not just incredible amounts of snow, but deep-freezing temperatures. From what the meteorologists are telling us, this storm is likely to get worse."

CHAPTER TWELVE

Ellen, Sarah, and I were having coffee in my office. Ellen had just returned from the studio after her show.

"At Homeland Security, we're used to making things happen," I said. "Make a phone call and stuff falls into place. But this storm makes it impossible to plan ahead. Thank God we have a tough, decisive president, but even Matt Blake is challenged by this monster storm."

"Fortunately, we have apartments here at Federal Plaza," Sarah said. "I don't see any of us going anywhere tonight. Even though you and Ellen live just a few blocks from here, I don't think you want to risk getting stuck in a snowdrift. I don't know how Ellen is going to handle her show tomorrow."

"The execs at NBC are pretty ingenious," Ellen said. "They've taped a show where a video of the host was shown on the TV while the interviews were conducted by telephone. Based on what the mayor said, I don't want to get stuck in a drift or risk a felony conviction by trying to get to the studio."

"Well, I think it's about time we break for dinner," I said. "The kitchen is very well stocked with food for a situation like this."

"How about booze?" Sarah asked.

"Yes, we have plenty," I said as I walked over to a cabinet that also served as a makeshift bar. "Let's toast to the meteorologists of the world. They're going to need some luck after this mess is over."

The three of us had a quiet dinner in my private dining room. The room overlooked the New York City Civic Center, normally a bustling area surrounded by government buildings. The strange view was pure white with the blizzard still swirling snow in every direction. The Beatles song, *Hey Jude* played in a nearby office, a song I always loved. Given our circumstances *Helter Skelter* would have been more appropriate.

***

My apartment at 26 Federal Plaza is far from unpleasant, even though it's a government facility. At 1,250 square feet, with two bedrooms and two bathrooms, it's a perfect size for Ellen and me. The walls were painted a soft taupe, not government gray, and the furniture included a plush leather couch and rich mahogany cabinets, giving the place a warm feeling. Maybe it was the weird excitement of being stuck in a blizzard in July, but Ellen and I both felt horny as hell. We showered together and forgot about the weather.

CHAPTER THIRTEEN

Tuesday, July 18

The alarm rang at 5:30 a.m. I like to get a jump on the day, especially on a day when I didn't know what was about to jump on me. Adhering to Mayor Adams' recommendation to conserve energy, we again showered together.

"You're pretty frisky for a cabinet officer."

"Hey, we've got work to do," I said.

"Like what?" Ellen asked.

"Let's save up some fun for later," I said. "I want to see what your network has to say about the weather. I just looked out the window and I can't distinguish one shape from another. The snow hasn't let up a bit from what I can tell."

My phone rang, and Ellen picked up.

"It's the White House for you, honey."

"Good morning, Mr. President," I said.

"When I picked you to head up Homeland Security, Rick, I knew that one of your talents was your ability to communicate in front of a camera. Well, we need that talent right now. This snowstorm has gone from a curiosity to a danger in the past few hours. Don't lie to people but let them know that we have a handle on this situation, which we do—sort of. An hour ago, I mobilized the National Guard, and I'm about to call up the Army, which will drive a lot of pundits crazy, but national security is my most important job—and yours. You have an excellent broadcast studio there at Federal Plaza. I'll have the emergency management people email you an extensive list of talking points. Use it well, Rick."

"I spoke to Lester Ballard, Director of the National Weather Service, Mr. President. I didn't want to talk to Professor Peterson, the climate maven, but rather to a guy who looks at things objectively without hatching mad theories to attract grant money. Ballard had good news, or I should say as good as I can expect. He said that satellite data showed the storm was slowly moving from west to east, and the edge of the pattern was over Western Pennsylvania and slowly moving east. New York City could expect the snow to stop at around 11 p.m. tonight. He also said that temperatures should return to seasonal normal by tomorrow morning, normal being in the 70s and 80s. He didn't have to tell me what would come next—massive flooding from the melting snow. I'll call you later to give you an update, Mr. President."

Ellen's producer called and told her that NBC had lined up another climate change expert who also happens to be a meteorologist. The forecast called for the storm to intensify during the day before gradually stopping tonight. NBC requested that Ellen be able to use the TV studio at 26 Federal Plaza rather than trying to trudge uptown to NBC. It was my decision to make and I okayed it because I thought Ellen's show would be important for the nation. But to avoid the appearance of impropriety that I loaned federal property to my wife, we charged NBC the same amount they would have to pay to rent any off-premise studio.

My address to the nation was scheduled for 12:30 p.m. to give networks enough lead time to shuffle around their current programming so they could air my talk. The program would be a modified press briefing, with reporters from the major news outlets allowed to call in.

Charlene Devitt, my press aide, stood before the camera to introduce me. Charlene, at a mere five feet, is articulate and photogenic, although she needs to stand on a platform to be seen by the camera. She has medium length blond hair, which she styles to look like Dana Perino, TV commentator and former press aide to President George W. Bush. Charlene's a big fan of Ellen and would love to have her own show some day.

"Ladies and gentlemen, it's my privilege to introduce Rick Bellamy, Secretary of Homeland Security."

"Good afternoon everyone," I said. I never say 'my fellow Americans' because that's a phrase that tradition reserves for the President of the United States.

"I never thought that the weather would be a subject for Homeland Security, but then I never imagined a weather system like the one we're experiencing. Records the world over have been shattered by this amazing blast of arctic air in mid-July. We all remember as short a time ago as Sunday morning—just two days ago—when we were all complaining about an uncomfortable heat wave. The heat wave suddenly became a cold wave, and soon we had to endure the blizzard that's still dumping snow across the nation and parts of the world as I speak. President Blake, as you've probably heard, has declared a National State of Emergency. As you've been hearing from local weather forecasters all morning, the National Weather Service predicts that an end is in sight, and we hope to see the blizzard stopping about 11 p.m. in the Eastern United States. So, what does this have to do with Homeland Security? The simple answer is that this unique weather has set up dangerous conditions across the nation. Besides the good news that the snow will finally stop falling tonight, we also hear that normal summer temperatures will resume, possibly tomorrow. I don't have to tell you what that means—flooding like our country has never experienced before. I have a request, on behalf of the President of the United States, that we all pull together as a nation of individuals dedicated to seeing an end to this shock. Please don't simply cooperate with law enforcement and first responders, but be ready to assist in any way you can. Together we can prevent this calamity from turning into a disaster."

Ellen walked up to me as I was being unhooked from the sound system.

"I'm not the only TV star in the family," she said. "You were perfect and hit just the right pitch. I think a lot of people are breathing easier after listening to you. My producer has a request. Could you make an appearance on my show this afternoon? I'll go over the questions I'll ask you beforehand. I think it's important that our viewers hear some further words from my handsome hubby."

"Of course, babe, I'd be happy to. But let me ask you a couple of questions about your other guests. Who are they and what will they be talking about?"

"You know Al Roker, the NBC meteorologist. Al, with his great sense of humor, helps to set the right tone for people to hear troublesome news. The next guy is a bit controversial. His name is Nigel Deming, an Englishman and meteorologist. The sum and substance of his appearance will be that he agrees with Professor Peterson, the climate maven. Deming thinks that we're seeing a brand-new phenomenon that's never happened before, but it's still a matter of climate change."

"In other words, bullshit."

"Afraid so."

CHAPTER FOURTEEN

"Welcome to *The Ellen Bellamy Show*. I'm your host, Ellen Bellamy, and I'm cautiously optimistic that we may be looking forward to some promising weather news for later tonight. As you've probably heard by now, the National Weather Service announced that the snow will begin to taper off, and the storm should move off the east coast around 11 tonight. This afternoon's show will continue with our favorite topic—the weather. Here in Manhattan, the accumulation has hit 10 feet and is still mounting. The sanitation department is begging and pleading with everyone not to drive. The mayor has announced that it's a felony to drive a non-emergency vehicle without permission of the Office of Emergency Management.

"Our special guest today is Nigel Deming, a meteorologist from England, who has an interesting view on these freezing temperatures and the snowfall. But first we'll break for a couple of commercials that will advertise some ways to beat the heat. Hopefully, we'll be able to use their advice soon."

Many advertisers didn't get a chance to change their ads, and half of the commercial spots did, as Ellen predicted, talk about ways to beat the heat, including commercials for air conditioners and deck awnings. As the break ended, Ellen introduced Deming.

"Hello everyone," Deming said. "Yesterday, Ellen hosted a gentleman named Dwight Peterson, a professor and climate expert. He announced the controversial idea that this weather event may be caused by a sudden quickening of climate change. I'm a meteorologist, not a climate expert. I study matters that are close at hand, not long-range changes in climate. But I must say from my many years of experience, that climate change is accelerating at a blazingly fast pace. As President Blake said recently, this frightening weather will be something we'll study for a long time before we come up with any definitive answers."

"But Mr. Deming," Ellen said, "even though you can't come up with a definitive answer, do you have a theory as to what may be going on?" *If not, what the hell are you doing on my show?*

"Ellen, I've looked at the opinions of every climate expert and meteorologist, and I'm convinced that climate change *is* the culprit, but the world has never seen this phenomenon before. I believe, ruling out all other possible causes, that the origin of this event occurred in space, possibly outer space. I don't know how, but I believe that something strange is happening to the rays of the sun itself. I don't believe the problem originates here on earth, or even in our own atmosphere."

CHAPTER FIFTEEN

July 18 - Peoria, Illinois

"What the hell do you mean we've lost all power, Carol? We have a goddam new generator that cost a fortune. Did you call the electricians?"

"Our phones are out, including cell phones. I've never seen anything like this, Janet. I just heard a report on the radio—a battery powered-radio—that half of Peoria is without electricity, including City Hall. Just look out the window. According to the guy on the radio, our infrastructure just isn't designed for something like this. The heating system just crapped out, along with the electricity and the emergency generator."

Janet Munson is the executive director of the Pleasant Fields Nursing Home in Peoria, Illinois. She retired from the Army three years before with the rank of colonel. She commanded a tank battalion in Iraq, and she has a reputation for her military can-do attitude.

"I don't give a flying fuck what the guy on the radio says. We have 140 elderly people in this place, people who depend on us to take care of them. That's why we've invested so much money in this building—to make sure it's up and running no matter what the weather is. These people need us. We can't just say, 'Oh gee, the shitty weather means you're going to freeze to death.' The freezing temperatures, not to mention the blizzard, are screwing everything up, We're out of communication and out of power."

Carol Johnston, Janet Munson's assistant, was used to dealing with her demanding boss. She admired Munson's dedication to her work, but sometimes you come up against a brick wall, and that's exactly what happened to them.

Twenty-five visiting relatives were in the building, people who wanted to know what management was doing for their loved ones.

"Carol, I'm sorry to be cracking your ass with a whip, but we can't just sit here and do nothing. Did you send the aides around with extra blankets?"

"Yes, I also put all water taps on a trickle. If our pipes freeze we're really in trouble. The temperature inside the building is 48 degrees and dropping steadily."

"Grab a couple of aides and go room to room to ask the visitors to gather in the reception area. I want to shoot straight with these people. This isn't just a customer service issue—it will soon be a fucking matter of life and death."

Carol Johnston and her assistants rounded up all 25 of the visitors and asked them to report to the front reception hall. Janet Munson stood before the group.

"I've gotten to know many of you over the past few months, and I think you know me as a straight shooter. We have a problem, all of us. My job as the head of this place is to take care of your loved ones, and that's exactly what I intend to do. But I can't minimize the trouble we're in. We're out of communication and out of power. As you all know if you read our newsletter a couple of months ago, the board decided to invest a hell of a lot of money on a state of the art emergency generator, even though we already had a pretty good one. Well, the damn thing's down along with everything else. As a lot of you know I once commanded a tank battalion in Iraq when I was in the Army. In a matter of minutes, I could round up a few dozen tanks and charge out to kick some jihadi ass. But now, for one of the few times in my life, I feel like I've run out of options. I like to think that I can handle anything, but I've never anticipated a freezing blizzard in July. The guy on the radio pointed out the obvious. Our infrastructure isn't designed for this shit, pardon my language."

"Janet," a man named Kirk Burton said, "I think I speak for everybody here, that we appreciate the problem we're all in. I couldn't have dreamed of a better place for my mom to be cared for than this well-run home. Don't blame yourself for the craziest weather any of us has ever seen. I have a Humvee which is great in bad weather. I'm going to venture out and see if I can contact your electricians. I know where their shop is located."

"Thanks, Kirk. It's what I expect of a good guy like you. But the people on the radio are screaming for their listeners to stay off the roads unless it's an emergency."

"There are about 140 patients here, Janet, and soon it will be freezing. I think that constitutes an emergency. After I visit the electricians' shop I'll go to the police station and alert them."

"I have a couple of two-way radios in my car, Kirk," another visitor said. "At least you'll be able to contact us."

***

Kirk Burton slowly maneuvered his Humvee down the snow-covered streets, occasionally blinded by the swirling blizzard. As he drove over a short bridge that traversed a creek, his vehicle suddenly swerved from a sudden blast of wind. Under the snow was a layer of black ice. His Humvee slammed into a wooden rail, cracking it in half, and then plunged into the 10-foot-deep creek. Burton's frozen body was discovered two weeks later.

CHAPTER SIXTEEN

Saturday, July 15 – Before the Cold Wave

On Saturday, July 15, the Great Lakes cruise ship *Victory 1* cast off its lines from its berth in Chicago. The itinerary would take the ship through all five of the Great Lakes and would tie up in Toronto 10 days later. Bill and Melissa Thompson of Philadelphia were celebrating their 35th wedding anniversary. Their daughter, Ellen Bellamy, gave them the cruise as an anniversary present. The ship was scheduled to leave on July 23, but a scheduling mistake changed its sailing time to July 15, which was just fine with the Thompsons. The idea of cruising on the Great Lakes seemed like a great way to escape the record heat wave. It was 95 degrees in Chicago on the day they sailed.

Victory 1 was a paddle-wheel cruise ship, but, like most modern paddle wheelers, its main propulsion came from standard underwater propellers, with minimal power from the paddle wheel. The paddle provided a great atmospheric effect, sort of like cruising in the old days. The ship was small compared to many cruise ships afloat, with a crew of 84 and 202 staterooms. Its modest size enabled it to easily navigate canals, locks, tranquil bays, and hidden ports where larger ships dare not go.

As they walked along the promenade deck after lunch, Bill looked at his watch.

"Hey, it's almost time for *The Ellen Bellamy Show*."

"The show doesn't air on weekends, remember?"

"Oh, right. Let's go inside anyway. It's hotter than hell on deck even with the breeze off the lake."

Like his daughter, Bill was an architect, although he didn't win the kinds of awards like Ellen did. Melissa was a dermatologist. Their main hobby was following the illustrious career of their famous daughter. They loved Ellen and the feeling was mutual.

***

At 9:15 a.m. on Sunday morning, July 16, they had just finished breakfast and were sipping coffee. The ship steamed north on Lake Michigan, headed for the Straits of Mackinac and then on to Lake Huron. They were about 40 miles from the Straits of Mackinac, cruising at a pleasant 15 knots. It was still hot as hell.

"Let's take a walk around deck," Bill said. "If we don't exercise we'll both gain 20 pounds with all the food they shove at you."

They had just rounded the deck near the bow and stopped to enjoy the breeze.

"Holy shit, what's that?" Bill yelled.

"God almighty, it's cold," Melissa said. "This is impossible. A minute ago we were sweating."

"Well, it feels like the impossible just happened. Let's get inside."

"Ladies and gentlemen, this is Captain Mike Pettibone speaking. Those of us on the ship's bridge are just as stumped as you are. I suggest looking at the reports coming in on the TV."

The Thompsons went to their stateroom and channel-surfed from one news show to another. The Sunday morning talk shows were put on hold to enable reporters to try to explain the amazing change in the weather.

What had been a smooth cruise a few minutes before, started to become rocky. The captain slowed the ship to 10 knots to accommodate the growing mountains of waves. It began to snow, and the wind howled at 50 mph.

"What the hell is that?" yelled Doug Stewart, the first officer. "It feels like we just dropped an anchor."

The wind and rising seas splashed water on the paddle wheel, which soon became encased in ice, freezing it in place. Instead of assisting in propulsion, the wheel acted like a giant anchor, slowing the ship to a nauseating 5 knots, nauseating because the waves hammered the ship from all sides. At 22,000 square miles Lake Michigan is a large body of water. It is known to get rough at times, but neither the captain nor the first officer had ever seen such oceanlike waves that battered the ship.

The captain ordered all passengers to get inside, not that anybody needed his advice. The freezing wind and pounding waves spoke for themselves. The air temperature was 20 degrees Fahrenheit, with a wind chill well below zero.

A few of the passengers packed sweaters, but most only brought summer clothes. The ship was equipped with a heating system, but the large number of broken windows kept the temperature down. A few of the crew busied themselves boarding up the windows that had blown out.

Because the captain was having a difficult time steering the ship, the result was sickening and constant rolls. Smashing glassware and toppling pots and pans made the scene even more chaotic. Walking across a room was an athletic endeavor.

"Captain, there's a problem with the main engine. I don't know if it's the high seas or the sudden drop in temperature, but the engine isn't giving us the power we need for steerage. I hate to say this, but we're a cork in the middle of a stormy lake."

The upper decks of the ship were equipped with heating wires to prevent the vessel from becoming top heavy with ice, even though the itinerary seldom called for cruises after Columbus Day in October. But the heating system was not enough to cope with the sudden drop in temperature.

Thick ice began to form along all exposed outer decks.

"Doug, if the ice continues to thicken along the upper decks we're as good as fucking sunk. Call the Coast Guard."

First Officer Stewart tuned the radio to the emergency channel.

"Mayday, mayday, mayday, this is American cruise ship *Victory 1* in northern Lake Michigan. Come in please." He then read the coordinates of the ship's position.

"Read you loud and clear, *Victory*. This is Captain James Hennessy of the Coast Guard Cutter *Moneghan*. We're about five miles south of your position. Describe your problem, captain, over."

"This is Captain Pettibone. Our ice mitigation system isn't working and our upper weather decks are becoming encrusted. Also, our main engine is down. We have no steerage. I'm concerned that we're going to founder. How many people can the *Moneghan* accommodate?"

"We can only take on an additional 75 people, captain. How many do you have aboard?"

"Counting the crew we have 590 people aboard. I'm preparing our life rafts now, but the people won't last long in a lifeboat in this weather, over."

"I'm closing on your position as soon as possible, but we can't go much faster with these waves. I've alerted the Coast Guard Station in Waukegan. Two large cutters are based there. I've told them to carry a minimal crew so they can accommodate the survivors from the *Victory*, over."

Survivors? Captain Pettibone's stomach took a turn when he heard that word.

"Please hurry, Captain Hennessey. I don't know how many more rolls my ship can take before she founders, over."

"Ladies and gentlemen, this is Captain Pettibone speaking. I would like to say some soothing words, but I can't. Our condition is critical. I've alerted the crew to assist all passengers to abandon ship. Your one and only goal is to climb into a lifeboat as a crewmember directs you."

Bill and Mellissa Thompson staggered down a passageway to their lifeboat station. The winds and seas had calmed down in the past 15 minutes, but the ship was still taking dangerous rolls. They came upon an elderly couple trying to walk a straight line.

"Let's help these two, hon," Bill said. "They can't make it to a boat on their own."

They each stood beside the two and gently walked them toward the launch platform. It was comforting to see three large Coast Guard cutters standing off to starboard. A gush of water droplets splashed them as a wave broke against the ship's hull. They were surprised that the water didn't hurt them, as the temperature of Lake Michigan, especially after the July heat wave, was still relatively warm compared to the wind and snow.

The Thompsons helped their new/old friends climb aboard the lifeboat.

***

"Rick, I think we should watch this report on the TV."

"Good afternoon, ladies and gentlemen, Monica Jackson for NBC News coming to you from the United States Coast Guard Station in Waukegan, Illinois. The scene here can best be described as happy bedlam, happy because what looked like a looming tragedy, had a good ending. Earlier we had reported that the beautiful Great Lakes paddle-wheel cruise ship, the *Victory 1*, got blindsided by this insane weather as the ship steamed toward the Straits of Mackinac on its way to Lake Huron. The upper decks became encased in heavy ice, and the main engine failed. Thanks to the fast action and courage of the crews of three Coast Guard cutters, all the crew and passengers of the *Victory 1* were rescued, with only a few people reporting minor injuries. It was not a moment too soon. Within minutes after the last person climbed aboard a lifeboat, the *Victory 1* foundered, capsized, and sank in 900 feet of water."

Monica Jackson walked across the room to a couple wrapped in a blanket, sipping coffee.

"I'm talking to a couple of passengers from Philadelphia, Bill and Melissa Thompson."

"Holy shit," Ellen screamed as she increased the volume on the TV. "They weren't scheduled to leave until the end of this week."

"We'd like to send our love to our wonderful daughter, Ellen Bellamy, who is actually a colleague of yours at NBC," Bill said. "We've been trying to call her, but, as you know, cell phone service is out. Ellen gave us this cruise as an anniversary present. So, thanks to you TV folks, we're able to send our love in person. Hey, Ellen, next time you book us on a cruise, can you arrange for better weather? Love you, baby. See you soon."

Any good producer knows that surprises make for great television. The photo of Monica Jackson's face would be printed and hung on the walls of NBC studios.

Ellen looked at her watch.

"I've got a show in 30 minutes, but I'm a fucking wreck."

"Hey, hon, don't be a wreck. Just thank God your folks are okay."

CHAPTER SEVENTEEN

Space Station *Stargazer*, July 18

"I don't think we were supposed to do what we did last night," Bill Cranston said to Nancy Mullin.

"Show me where there's a written regulation against it," she said. "Besides, don't you consider it an honor to be an astronaut who got a blow job in space?"

Cranston looked around jokingly in an exaggerated circle. "Are you sure there's nothing floating around," he said.

Nancy laughed.

"I'm very thorough when I need to be," she said with a wink. "Hey, we're both single and horny. Nothing wrong with a little zero-gravity sex."

"No, nothing wrong at all," Cranston said as he reached over and stroked her thigh. "Let's finish up today's chores so we can explore some more new worlds."

"You're on, cowboy."

Bill Cranston and Nancy Mullin are both former military officers.

Cranston was in the Marines, and Mullin in the Air Force, both having left active duty two years before. They were both 35 years old and each held the rank of captain when they left the service. Nancy Mullin stands at five feet nine, has short brown hair, and the figure of a gymnast, which she was at the Air Force Academy. Cranston is a big man at six feet two with a muscular build. He has blue eyes and sandy blond hair. The Rosetta Corporation hired them to work on *Stargazer*, the private space station that was owned by the company and controlled from its corporate headquarters in Billings, Montana. Like other space stations, *Stargazer* is equipped with minimal propulsion. It can't take off or land by itself. Service to the station, including resupply and crew changes, is accomplished by visits from rocket-launched replenishment pods. As of 2018 only two space stations are in orbit and operational, the *International Space Station*, or ISS, and *Stargazer*. Other space stations in the past include: China's *Tiangong-1* (defunct); and *Tiangong-2* (launched in September 2016, not permanently manned); *Skylab*; *Mir*; and the *Almaz* and *Salyut* series. *Stargazer* is similar in design to the *International Space Station*, ISS, on which the Rosetta Corporation was the major contractor. The station is 240 feet long, 370 feet wide, and 70 feet high. It can carry a crew of six, but is currently manned by only two astronauts, Mullin and Cranston. Nancy Mullin is the mission commander.

"Anything new on earth to change the subject to something less exciting?" Cranston asked.

"Still totally fucking weird, Bill. The last we heard from Montana was that the temperatures nationwide are still well below freezing, and the blizzard shows no signs of letting up. I'm glad I volunteered for this mission. Playing around with a handsome hunk like you beats the hell out of shoveling snow in July."

"Let's check on our newly-launched satellites," Cranston said. "Do you have any idea why we've launched so many? Twenty satellites seem like a hell of a lot for one company."

"Bill, I don't ask a lot of questions. Do you wonder why?"

"Yeah, why don't you ask questions? Lack of curiosity?"

"No, I'm curious as hell," Nancy said, "but last I checked I earn $305,000 a year, and I know that you earn the same. If they want to pay me that kind of money, I'm happy to keep my mouth shut as I've been politely requested to do. For that kind of dough, if it's legal, I'll do it."

"What if they want to make a video of you and me fooling around?"

"Make me an offer, big guy."

"Hey, let's get back to work," Bill said. "Headquarters wants us to send photos of earth. We also need to put each of the satellites through a round of tests. I wonder what these satellites are for."

"Like I said, Bill, I don't ask questions unless I have to. At $305K a year, I don't care if they use the satellites to raise chinchillas."

"I'm sending the earth photos to headquarters now," Bill said. "It sure as hell doesn't look like the earth we left behind. Instead of the beautiful colors, mainly blue, it now looks like a friggin snowball. Hey, stop that. Let's finish the tests first."

CHAPTER EIGHTEEN

July 19

The alarm went off at 5:30 a.m. and Ellen slept right through it. She was exhausted from back-to-back shows, each of which required extensive interviews with guests. She was still emotionally drained from seeing her parents being interviewed as disaster survivors.

I got out of bed as quietly as possible so as not to disturb her sleep. I walked over to the window, expecting to see our first morning in three days without snow. The weatherman got it wrong— again. It was still snowing like a pillow fight. The street scene in front of Federal Plaza looked like a snow-covered lawn. The snow was piled so deep that you couldn't tell if anything was under it, including vehicles.

I turned on the TV to get the latest weather report. Our friend Al Roker, the NBC meteorologist, was earning his large salary.

"Good morning folks," Roker said. "I fully expected to report a day without snow, but my expectation differs from reality. It's still coming down heavily, although we thought it would end last night at around eleven. It's now 6 a.m. and our winter wonderland in July continues without let-up. What shocks me is that our normal methods of predicting the weather are buried under snow, if you'll pardon the pun. The snow accumulation tally in Central Park is 14 feet—that's feet, not inches. My revised forecast calls for—and I can't believe I'm saying this—snow. Behind the front that caused all the snow was, you guessed it, another front. Normally, with Doppler radar and satellites we can see a front approaching way in advance, but these fronts move blindingly fast. To bring you some perspective from a different part of the world, I call on Nancy Drummond, our NBC reporter on assignment at Guantanamo Bay, Cuba."

"Good morning, Al. Nancy Drummond here, reporting from the American military base at Guantanamo Bay, Cuba. The normal temperature for this time of year is 95 degrees, but this is anything but normal. It's 25 degrees and snowing heavily here in the beautiful Caribbean. The accumulation so far is four feet, a bit more than expected for an area that *never* gets any snow at all. The number of prisoners in custody is currently 41. It took a lot of fast thinking to rearrange their accommodations to allow for heated living spaces. Follow the camera as we pan around the area near where I'm standing at the entrance to the prison. As you can see, the view is more like North Dakota in winter than Cuba in summer. That large mound of snow you see behind me contains a Humvee. I hope you weather forecasting people have some good news for us soon. Nancy Drummond reporting for *NBC News* from Guantanamo Bay, Cuba. Over to you, Al."

"We turn now to our NBC affiliate in Chicago. Reporter Frank Nuevez is on the scene."

"Good morning, Al, and good morning to NBC viewers wherever you are. Frank Nuevez here for *NBC News*. The Windy City in summer is typical of most northern cities—hot and humid. But as we all know, there's nothing typical about the past few days. The scene behind me looks like a snow-covered parkway, but it's not. I'm standing on the Wabash Avenue Bridge overlooking the Chicago River, which would normally be clogged with boats at this time of year. Well, it's still clogged with boats, but they're not going anywhere soon. The river is a link between the Great Lakes and the Gulf of Mexico, but for the past few days it's anything but a link. The Windy City is living up to its name, with gusts of 65 mph feeding the blizzard. Back to you, Al. Frank Nuevez reporting for *NBC News* in Chicago."

Nuevez is a big man at 6'4" and over 250 pounds. His size gave comfort to the viewers because his wind-whipped clothing made it look like he was about to be blown into the river.

CHAPTER NINETEEN

July 20 – 6:15 a.m.

Ellen walked up next to me in her bathrobe and handed me a cup of coffee. We stared at the white Manhattan cityscape when the phone rang. It was 6:15 a.m., July 20, the fourth day of the snowstorm.

"It's either the White House or your producer. I'm betting it's your producer," I said.

"Hi, Elliott, she's right here," I said, handing Ellen the phone.

"Not another climate change asshole," Ellen said. The foul-mouthed TV crowd was rubbing off on my normally soft-spoken Ellen.

"You know the guy, Ellen," O'Keefe said. "He was on your show just last week talking about the heat wave, then we had him back to talk about the blizzard. This will be a great contrast to hear him talk more about the deep freeze again after discussing the heat wave a few days ago. The last two shows from your husband's office worked great. The government is charging us a lot of money for use of the facilities, but it's worth it."

Ellen put down the phone and let out a sigh.

"You always tell me how even-tempered I am, hon, but I'm afraid I'll lose it if I have to interview another self-indulgent idiot who worships at the altar of climate change. Their message never changes no matter what the weather is. If it's warmer than usual, it's 'global warming.' If it's colder than usual, like now, it's 'climate change.' How can so many people be so full of shit? If you dare ask a question or raise doubts about a statistic, you're labeled as a 'climate change denier.'"

"Hey, hon," I said, "you didn't get to where you are by being a pussy cat. Follow your instincts, which are sharp as hell. If you have a question, ask it, and don't worry about repercussions. The American people need to know what's going on, and you're a major player in the game. You don't get those sky-high ratings because you're beautiful, even though you are. Remember, I was there when you blasted away a couple of terrorists with an AK-47. Pinning a tedious asshole to the wall should be easy."

"I'd rather shoot him," she said, laughing. "Will you and Sarah be next to the set watching the show?"

"Of course," I said. "Watching *The Ellen Bellamy Show* is the high point of our day. Don't you like having the Director of the FBI and the Secretary of Homeland Security in your corner?"

"Hey, I don't just want you two in my corner," Ellen said, "I want your honest feedback after the show. The climate change types like to play with bullshit. I don't, and I'm sure Sarah, you, and not to mention President Blake, all feel the same way. We need facts, not scientific poetry. I gotta take a shower and get ready for the show."

"I could use a shower too."

"Good idea, handsome. Take off that robe and follow me."

CHAPTER TWENTY

" A snowy July good afternoon, ladies and gentlemen, and welcome to
The Ellen Bellamy Show." That scar on her face from her childhood
accident is more like a dimple, and looked especially great on camera. I
think the makeup people recognize that too.

"I'm your host, Ellen Bellamy, and the subject of today's show is—you
guessed it—the weather. Before I introduce our guest, let's hear from our
smiley-faced NBC weatherman, Al Roker."

"Hi Ellen, and hello to our viewers," Roker said, "stuck in front of your
TVs because there's nowhere to go in this nonstop blizzard. I've been por-
ing over the weather charts and computer readouts all day, and I'm shocked
to say that I don't see any end to this mess. We thought we were able to
predict the end of the blizzard two nights ago, but daylight came along,
and the snow was still falling. A couple of our producers asked if I had an
excuse for not doing what I'm supposed to do—predict the weather. But
I can't. This morning I was on a conference call with meteorologists across
the country, including the National Weather Service, and we all agree on
one thing: we can't predict this weather pattern, at least not yet. So, my

forecast is this—no change in the weather. More snow is on the way unless we can find a scientifically accurate way to say otherwise. Over to you, Ellen."

"I don't often plug my colleagues on the show, but I have to say that Al Roker is one of the smartest people I know, and definitely the smartest meteorologist. If Al is stumped, so am I. Now it's my pleasure to introduce our special guest (*like it's really a pleasure to introduce a flaming asshole*), Professor Dwight Peterson of NOAA."

"Good afternoon, Ellen, and good afternoon to your viewers," Peterson said.

"Professor, please give us your take on the past 24 hours. Meteorologists nationwide predicted that the snow would end two nights ago. Well, as we all know, it didn't, and the blizzard continues without let-up."

Sarah Watson and I stood next to each other watching the taping. Because of the weather, Ellen interviewed her guest by telephone and a remote TV camera at his brother's apartment in upper Manhattan.

"This is all quite predictable, Ellen," Peterson said.

"It's a good thing Peterson is in a different location," Sarah said. "Judging from the look on Ellen's face, I think she would have slugged the guy just now."

"Predictable?" Ellen said, her voice close to maximum volume. "I remind you, professor, that last week—just a few days ago—you were on my show talking about the terrible heat wave, which you blamed on climate change, and you summarized your talk by saying that the heat wave was 'predictable.' So, what is it? Hot or cold?"

"It's all included in the pattern of climate, Ellen," Peterson said. "Global warming has many different faces."

"Global *warming*?" Ellen yelled (she actually yelled). Do I have to remind you that it's 15 fucking degrees Fahrenheit outside?"

Sarah leaned over to me and whispered, "I think that was alliterative brilliance the way Ellen worked in the word 'fucking' just before the word 'Fahrenheit.'"

I cracked up. "Hey, wise guy, listen to the show. I bet a couple of producers just had heart attacks over Ellen's losing it."

Ellen didn't apologize for her language (which NBC tradition would for years refer to as "the f-bomb heard round the world"). She just sat there waiting for Peterson to answer.

"Well, I grant you that it's cold outside."

"I'll take that admission as scientific progress," Ellen said, with a look that was even colder than the outside temperature.

"But you see," said the chastened-looking professor, "air temperature is a relative thing…"

"No, it isn't," Ellen said, immediately. "Fifteen degrees is fifteen degrees, and it's only relative to other numbers, and let me advise you that fifteen degrees is (*here comes another f-bomb, I thought*) seventeen degrees below freezing, Ikey, and that, sir, is known as cold."

The sound engineer was unable to block out the laughter and cheering on the set. She called the guy "Ikey," apparently thinking that he no longer deserved the title, "professor."

"But climate is vastly more complex than meteorology," Peterson said, looking like a dog that just crapped on the rug. "I took my PhD in climate studies because I thought meteorology was too simplistic. It's a highly complicated field, and I understand that you find it daunting." A snide swipe at Ellen's supposed thick-headedness.

"I've clocked as many classroom hours as you have, *professor*, although in fields that have answers to questions, like mathematics, engineering, and architecture. Please don't be condescending to me or our audience. Why don't you admit that you're spouting nonsense? Fifteen degrees Fahrenheit is cold, and 95 degrees, the temperature just before this cold wave, is hot. Most people do not have a hard time understanding that, and I recommend that you recognize it as well. Thank you for coming on my show." She didn't smile as she "thanked" him.

***

Ellen and I sipped coffee in my dining room after her show. At 5:25 in the evening, the daylight looked like afternoon, what you'd expect for mid-July. The snow was still coming down heavily.

"So, our English friend Nigel Deming is on board with most experts who think that this crazy weather is a result of climate change," Ellen said. "The only new thing that Deming brought to the game is his hunch that the climate change originates in space. I mean where the hell else would it originate, in a sewer?"

"I've had it up to my eyeballs with experts," I said. "What do *you* think?"

"I can't buy that this summer blizzard was caused by long-term changes in climate," Ellen said. "These 'climatistas' as they've been called, are in the business of promoting their theories and raking in grant money. Hey, I don't doubt that climate change is a real thing, and human activities are partly to blame, but to say that this sudden calamity is the sole result of climate change is nonsense. Do you think the way I handled Peterson will throw a wet blanket on the true believers who want to use my show to flex their brain-muscles?"

"I think any climate change expert you have on the show in the future will want to control the pause button," I said. "I've never been prouder of you. Most media stars just want to burnish their own reputations. You perform like a real journalist—You look for the truth, even if you use an f-bomb to seek it."

CHAPTER TWENTY ONE

"Hey, Rick. You said before that we're going to have a special guest for dinner tonight," Ellen said. "I'm up to my eyeballs with special guests. Please tell me it's not a climate change expert. Who is it?"

"Mike Watson, Sarah's husband," I said.

"What a great guy," Ellen said. "After his latest book, I think he's my favorite novelist. How did he get clearance from Emergency Management to come here?"

"Sarah called Emergency Management and asked to speak to the director himself. She ended the conversation with the words, 'I don't give a rat's ass what you have to do, just make it happen.' Sarah knows how to work around bureaucracies."

***

Mike and Sarah Watson came into the dining room at 6:15. I had met Mike a few times before, and I agree with Ellen that he's a great guy. He's 5'10," about 55 years old, slim, with sandy brown hair, and he's seems to be enthusiastic about everything. A few months ago, his latest novel, *The Deep River*, hit *The New York Times Best Seller List* at number three.

He grabbed my hand and pumped his usual handshake. Ellen and I congratulated him on making the best seller list, and he graciously thanked us. After dinner, we steered the conversation toward novel writing. We were both tired of talking about the weather, and so was Sarah.

"Mike," Ellen said, "tell us where you get your ideas for writing fiction. I've written a couple of non-fiction books on architecture that have done well, but I'd love to write a novel someday. Do your ideas just show up out of nowhere?"

"It's like Stephen King says, stories exist in the world like fossils, and it's the novelist's job to unearth them," Mike said. "I get my ideas from just looking, listening, and paying attention to the world around me. Suddenly, a story reveals itself. I come up with some characters and follow them as they create the scenes that make up the story. Last year I was fishing with a friend on his boat on a wide river near his house in Connecticut. When I asked him how deep the water was, he said fifty feet in spots. Ever since I almost drowned as a kid, I've been nervous around water. I was also aware that a story had showed up. *The Deep River* is about a guy who's afraid of water and finds himself alone on a small boat with no means of propulsion. I won't spoil it for you in case you read it."

"I read it and loved it," Ellen said. "I wish I had it with me for you to autograph."

"Don't worry, Ellen, I'll send you a signed copy as soon as delivery service starts up again."

"I wonder how you look at this weird weather we're having," I said. "I bet a story idea has come to you. I feel like I'm living as a character in a novel with this crap. It isn't the reality I'm used to, or the reality that any-body's used to."

"Yes, Rick, a story is definitely in the making. I'll share the plot with you, even though my agent would shoot me if he knew I told you about it."

"Please go on, hon," Sarah said. "We'd love to hear how you can explain this insanity using fiction."

"I often tell people that reality is overrated, and that's why I write novels," Mike said. "Well, the reality we're confronted with is stranger than any science fiction than I've ever written. I watched Ellen's show when she interviewed that climate-change fanatic and I thought she was great. That guy is better than me at fiction. So, how's this for a story line? One day during a heat wave with high temperature and humidity, the air suddenly starts to chill. Within a half hour, the temperature drops 50 degrees. The climate-change crowd closed ranks and started to chant that mankind has brought on the change in the weather by pumping carbon dioxide into the air, even though that's been happening for hundreds of years. Fiction, yes, but boring fiction, spouted by people who have an agenda to push. So, how's this for excitement? Maybe just as crazy as blaming the immediate weather on long-range trends, but I think it's a lot more interesting. In my story, the sudden drop in temperature is caused by a group of people who manipulate the weather *on purpose*, people who want to conquer the earth. They do this by refocusing the sun's rays so that the earth is deprived of normal solar warming. After they kill off all the inhabitants, the evil characters take over and return the atmosphere to normal. So how do you like it? My agent thought it was great."

There was silence around the table for an uncomfortable minute or so. I looked at Sarah, whose face indicated that she just heard something startling. I then looked at Ellen, who registered the same emotion.

"Hey, Mike," Ellen said. "You and I are married to a couple of high-placed government sceptics, but I get a feeling that they're still thinking about your story line. I know I am."

"Well, that's great news for my novel, but I'm afraid that I'm going to risk a bunch of readers tossing the book across the room. Science fiction is great, but it must be based on some known facts to be a believable story. I'm afraid that's as far as I've gotten with my story, because my research showed me that the idea just doesn't work. We keep trying to manipulate weather, but it works only in small increments. A lot of well-meaning scientists are studying the idea of changing the weather, but they keep coming up empty. So that's the excitement of creating fiction. I just make up new facts. In the case of science fiction, it's easy. I just create a new thing, or process, or method, or species. It lets the reader know that it's a 'made-up' fact, and it's time to keep reading."

"Mike has a PhD in physics from Cal Tech, and all of his fans know that. So, if he makes up some science, who's to argue?" Sarah said.

"Unfortunately, we don't get to make up stories here in reality," I said. "We have to take what's there and live with it."

"But there's a big exception in reality," Mike said. "Occasionally something new comes along that we never knew about. What if this unique weather event was caused by something we never knew existed?"

"So where does that leave us?" Ellen asked.

"Where I always leave you," Mike said. "Buy my next book to find out."

CHAPTER TWENTY TWO

July 21

"Do you realize that whenever people hear the name Rosetta Corporation they'll laugh," said Frank Morgan, CEO of Rosetta to his operations VP, Phil Duncan. Today is July 21 and it's been snowing for five fucking days. We're used to seeing weather like this—in January. Not only has it been snowing for five days, but I've been waiting for an answer for that long. What the hell happened?"

Phil Duncan had been with Rosetta since he finished graduate school at MIT with a Master's Degree in aeronautical engineering at the age of 23. He's now 45 and is senior in command after Frank Morgan. Duncan is 5'10" and about 20 pounds overweight. He has a receding hairline which he tries to mask with a comb-over. He blows his nose constantly out of habit whether he needs to or not.

Frank Morgan was formerly an Air Force general and a NASA astronaut. Rosetta's mission is to use satellites for communications as well as weather monitoring. Rosetta has more satellites in orbit than any other private firm.

"Frank, you know I'm not a bullshitter, so I won't start now. I haven't the foggiest idea what happened. Not only that, I have no idea what *will* happen. I'm as much in the dark as anybody. I met with all five department heads this morning, and nobody knows what's going on. We've run engineering tests on all our major systems and everything checks out okay. I spoke to our two astronauts on *Stargazer* and they're going through their usual system and satellite tests. They report no problems. We're dealing with something that none of us understands and we've got to admit something—we may have nothing to do with this. It could be pure coincidence."

"Phil," Morgan said, "you may not be a bullshitter, but the report you've just given me is pure bullshit and you know it. This strange weather began within 15 minutes after one of our major satellite tests, the one where we also tested the solar panels. You can't tell me that's pure coincidence."

Rosetta Corporation is listed on the New York Stock Exchange and is considered one of the leading defense contractors in the country. Morgan began expanding Rosetta's mission 10 years ago, to concentrate more on civilian uses of satellite technology. He assembled a team of scientists that the *Wall Street Journal* calls the "smartest bunch of technologists in American industry." Morgan prides himself on his fanatical attention to detail. He once began a corporate meeting by predicting that one of Rosetta's satellites was degrading in orbit and would soon burn up. Nobody in the meeting agreed with him. The satellite entered the earth's atmosphere and disintegrated before the meeting was over. If there is one thing that Morgan hates above all else, it's not knowing the answer to why a problem has occurred.

"Frank, I gotta believe this problem is a pure coincidence and has nothing to do with our satellites. If we were somehow involved, we'd know why and what happened. As of right now we know less than a local meteorologist knows."

"Do you recommend that we contact NASA or Homeland Security?" Morgan asked.

"We could contact them, but we'd have nothing to say. I recommend that we say nothing, because that's exactly what we have to tell them."

"Phil, what about the problem that the astronauts reported with the retractable solar panels on one of our satellites? It happened close in time to the big weather event."

"The problem lasted just a few seconds, Frank. They think that some space junk may have hit one of the panels. But the panel retracted, and no further problem was reported."

"I may just be pissing into the wind," Morgan said, "but I want you to order another panel retraction test of all of our satellites."

"Well, we don't have to worry about pissing into the wind, Frank, because the tests will be performed in space."

"Very funny, wiseass. Let me know as soon as the test results are in."

CHAPTER TWENTY THREE

July 22

"You know, Bill, we've been doing things backwards," Nancy Mullin said.

"What do you mean? Are you questioning my engineering expertise?"

"No, I mean you and me. Normally two single people meet, feel attracted to one another, then like each other, fall in love, and have sex. We started with the sex before we barely knew one another. Now, I feel like, I don't know, I'm really starting to like you—a lot. We've been screwing like a couple of lab rats, and I feel more strongly about you each time."

"I feel the same way about you, Nance. How about a kiss."

"I feel like taking a shower," Nancy said. "A more imaginative designer would have included a cylindrical shower for two. It would save energy."

Showering in space takes some getting used to as many astronauts have said. It's not really a shower because water in an anti-gravity environment tends to stick to your skin. A towel soaked with water is the substitute for a shower.

"Why don't you go wash up and I'll follow you. Then we'll play Scrabble like we planned."

"Why don't we decide on what game we'll play later," Nancy said. "Scrabble isn't doing it for me."

After they "showered," Bill pulled down the zipper on Nancy's suit, as Nancy did the same with his. They held each other, caressing in the weightless environment of the space station. *"Stargazer, Stargazer"* came the voice over the radio, "this is Rosetta Headquarters, come in please."

"This is *Stargazer*, read you loud and clear, Rosetta," Nancy said breathlessly.

"You sound like you're out of breath, Nancy," Phil Duncan said. "Everything okay?"

"Yes," she gasped, "Oh, my God, yes, yes, yes. I was just having a workout—on the treadmill."

"Frank Morgan wants you to perform the satellite tests again. I know it's time-consuming, but the boss man wants it."

"Oh shit, I mean of course," Nancy said. "We'll start right now."

"Why don't you finish your workout, Nancy," Duncan said, stifling a laugh. "You'll be fresh and alert for performing the tests."

"Oh, yes we will," Nancy panted, "Oh, wow, will we ever."

***

Bill and Nancy began the monotonous tests of the 20 Rosetta satellites. They began the procedure by sending a series of signals to each satellite, deploying the retractable solar panels. Each satellite is round and measure six feet in diameter. One by one, they extended the retractable rods containing the solar panels. Once the rod was extended, the solar panel would unfold. Their orders were to leave all solar panels in a deployed position until the final satellite was tested. Each test took seven minutes, so the entire operation would take 140 minutes. Then the solar panels on each of the satellites would be retracted, a five-minute operation per panel, adding another 100 minutes to the project.

"What the hell is going on?" Bill asked. "The solar panels are rotating on their own. They won't respond to the signal."

"Let me try the override protocol," Nancy said. "It must be a malfunctioning relay."

"All of the panels seem to be turned to the same direction," Bill said. "I thought they put in a fail-safe mechanism to prevent that."

"Why the hell are they facing the same way?" Nancy asked. "Nobody has ever given me an explanation for that. Like I've said many times, I don't ask too many questions."

"Those panels are the most powerful solar arrays in existence," Bill said. "If the panels all face in the same direction, they concentrate the sun's energy, which is what seems to have happened. Headquarters doesn't like to take chances, and that's why they put it the fail-safe—the fail-safe that failed."

"I designed the fail-safe system," Nancy said. "I can't understand why it's not working. I designed it to work—without fail. The override seems to be doing the trick. I just hope that the few minutes of concentrated sun rays on the solar panels didn't fuck anything up."

CHAPTER TWENTY FOUR

July 23

"Lilly Morton, reporting for *NBC News* here in cold and blustery Fort Lauderdale, Florida, where the unbelievable blizzard continues without a stop. Under that mountain of snow behind me is the building that houses the NBC studio."

Lilly Morton was standing out in the open to make a visual display of the blowing snow. She was dressed in arctic weather gear which she had a hard time finding in Fort Lauderdale.

"The temperature in Fort Lauderdale on this 23rd day of July is a balmy 22 degrees. Some homeowners here in Southern Florida, trying to save money, never bothered to equip their homes with central heating. It's either air conditioning or room temperature, whatever it may be. Frozen and burst pipes are being reported by the thousands."

As if a switch were thrown, the snow stopped, and a bright sun appeared. Lilly Morton stood before the camera with a confused look on her face. She put her hand to her forehead in a salute to block the sunrays.

"Hey, what the hell is going on?" she said, as a producer screamed in her ear for using the word "hell." She tucked the microphone under her arm to free up her hands to open her winter parka. "I'm stumped, folks. As you can see, the snow suddenly stopped falling and the sun is out. I'm looking at a thermometer on the building next to me, and it reads 82 degrees. Just a few minutes ago it was 22 degrees."

Morton disappeared from the camera screen. The abrupt rise in temperature caused her to faint and collapse into a mound of snow. Assistants from the studio ran to her aid and she revived within half a minute.

"Lilly's awake and doing just fine, folks," said Bob Housman, her stand-in. The producer told Housman to sign off and pass the show to the main studio in New York.

"I'm signing off for now and handing the report to the main NBC studio in New York. Over to you, Al," Housman said.

"Al Roker here for NBC in New York City. I'm told that Lilly Morton, our reporter in Fort Lauderdale, is doing fine after her fainting spell. I almost fainted myself. I think I'm here, but I'm not sure. Eight days ago, we began the strangest series of weather reports imaginable, with a gigantic blizzard of historic proportions in mid-July. Suddenly, and I do mean suddenly, the snow stopped, and the sun came out. For those of you who were watching, you just saw Lilly Morton, our reporter in Fort Lauderdale, Florida. She was freezing her butt off a couple of minutes ago, standing in the middle of swirling snow. Now the sun is shining brightly, and I've just been informed that the temperature there is 94 degrees, normal for this time of year in Fort Lauderdale, but at the same time *not normal* because it happened in the middle of a snow storm. Here in mid-town Manhattan we're also having ourselves yet another weather freak-out. As you can see, I'm standing here on the building plaza in my shirtsleeves and wearing a ball cap because of the bright sun. I'm still surrounded by mountains of snow, but the temperature is 86 degrees, and those mountains are starting to melt. We're monitoring the weather across the country and here's where I say let's have a look at 'your neck of the woods.' I've been saying that for so long it's become part of my personality. You folks have known me for a long time, and you know that I don't play games with you. But let me say this: Something is going on, and I'm beginning to think it's not an accident."

CHAPTER TWENTY FIVE

July 24

Frank Morgan, entered Rosetta's communications room, slamming the door against a wall.

"Precisely, what the fuck is going on?" Morgan shouted, his face a bright red.

Phil Duncan, the operations VP, walked up to him. Morgan valued Phil Duncan, not just for his executive skills, which were considerable, but for his willingness to get into Morgan's face when he was about to make an asshole of himself, which he did quite often in the past few days.

"I suppose this is just another coincidence," Morgan said to Duncan.

"Frank," Duncan said, "remember that it was *your* idea to run through another series of solar panel tests on all of our satellites, even though we had some doubts after the first incident. We were worried about the fail-safe system malfunctioning. Well, it happened again. I just spoke to Nancy Mullin on the *Stargazer*. She went through the override protocol and that seemed to undo the problem, but the solar panels were all faced in the same direction for quite a few minutes. We have no idea what that situation could result in, but we have yet another strange weather event. A half hour ago the temperature here in Billings was 19 degrees. Now it's 85 degrees."

"How the hell could that be?"

"Frank, the answer is that we don't know," Duncan said. He sat down on the office couch. "What we do know is that within minutes of our last two satellite tests, the world's weather went crazy. I've grilled every scientist and engineer who works for us, and not one of them has an answer."

"So, let's get this straight, Phil," Morgan said. "We perform a simple test of the satellites' solar panels, and the system goes apeshit, facing all of the panels in one direction, which apparently resulted in a radical weather change, although we have no idea how. Our fail-safe mechanism failed both times. Shit, fail-safe systems aren't supposed to fail. If it weren't for Nancy Mullin's quick thinking with the override switches, God knows what would have happened."

"The legal department thinks we should alert the government with our concerns," Morgan said.

"Here's an idea, Frank. Why don't I open a conversation with Rick Bellamy, Secretary of Homeland Security? We know each other from college, and we still correspond occasionally around the holidays. He's a good friend. Also, he's got the ear of President Blake."

***

"There's a man named Phil Duncan on line three for you, Rick," my assistant said. "He says you know him."

"He's an old college buddy," I said. "Good guy, but I don't have time to shoot the shit now."

"He says it's urgent, sir."

"Hi Phil, it's Rick. My assistant says something's urgent."

"I would normally ask to meet you in person with a matter like this, Rick, but we wanted to contact you right away. Are we on a secure line?"

"Yes, feel free to talk, Phil. What's up?"

"I'm going to put you on speaker. I'm with Frank Morgan, CEO of Rosetta."

"Good morning, Mr. Secretary," Morgan said. "Thank you for taking our call. I have a reputation for speaking in blunt language, sir, and I'm too old to change it. So rather than toss a bunch of legal bullshit at you, please let me get right to the point. As you know, Rosetta has 20 satellites in orbit. Their function is to enhance GPS capabilities, as well as perform some new sophisticated weather tracking. Well, sir, we ran a test of the solar panels on all the satellites eight days ago. One of the systems malfunctioned. Within a few minutes we experienced a historic weather anomaly. This morning we ran another series of tests. We encountered the same system malfunction but were able to override it. It took about 15 minutes to rearrange the solar panels. Within minutes, we experienced this morning's sudden end to the blizzard and return to normal temperatures. So, in summary, we performed two series of tests and simultaneously the world experienced two shocking weather changes. Our people can't come up with an explanation for what occurred, but it seems that the two incidents are too close in time to be mere coincidences."

I looked out the window as the sky darkened, signaling an incoming storm. Then I glanced at a building that displayed a digital date and temperature read-out. The temperature was 32 degrees and falling. A couple of minutes before it was 84 degrees.

"Mr. Morgan, I'm sorry to interrupt you, but can you tell me what the weather is right now in Montana."

"Well, the sky is darkening like a storm is coming," Morgan said.

"What's the temperature?" I asked.

Duncan called up the local weather on his cell phone.

"Holy shit," Morgan said "Sorry, Mr. Secretary. It's 27 degrees and dropping. Déjà vu all over again. It's starting to snow like a bitch."

"Here too," I said. "Mr. Morgan, I thank you for being a stand-up American for bringing this problem to us. I'm going to contact NOAA and put some senior people in touch with you. If something is causing this, whether it's a malfunctioning panel on your satellites or something else, there's a technical problem that you haven't figured out yet. And if it's a technical problem, there must be a technical solution."

God willing, I thought.

CHAPTER TWENTY SIX

July 24

"Good afternoon, ladies and gentlemen, and welcome to *The Ellen Bellamy Show*. I know that you're all fond of my charming spontaneity, but I have a confession to make, although I'm sure you're aware of it. Like most TV shows, *The Ellen Bellamy Show* is taped before the show runs. In the past few days, however, it's been different. Because of yesterday's wacky weather event, when the snow stopped and the temperatures soared, if we showed you what we taped it would have been totally inaccurate. As you know, the temperatures once again reversed, and it's well below freezing across the country. So, I'm speaking to you live, which I find a little intimidating. If I make a mistake, please don't flame me on Facebook.

"Before I continue with the show, I have an important announcement that the government requested I make. This morning's rapid climb in temperature resulted in some fast melting of snow. Then, the thermometer reversed, and we were again plunged into a deep freeze. The result? Black ice. Wicked, nasty black ice, the likes of which you've never seen before. Hospitals are reporting a rash of fractured limbs from people slipping and falling. So, if you must venture out, please be careful."

The TV went blank, along with all the lights in the building. Ellen was still broadcasting from 26 Federal Plaza, and she assumed that such a critical government location would have immediate power backup. I had been standing 20 feet from the soundstage as I always did for Ellen's show. Sarah Watson stood next to me.

An assistant groped his way through the darkness to remove the cover over the window that had been put in place to block the sun before each broadcast.

Sarah Watson and I walked over to Ellen. I lighted our way with the flashlight app on my cell phone.

"I was worried about this," I said. "With the temperature extremes we were bound to have a power blackout."

As I said that the lights came back on, powered by the building's emergency generator.

"The power should have come on within a split second," I said to Sarah Watson.

"I'll have the maintenance crew check it out," Watson said. "This is unacceptable, but the way the thermometer skyrocketed and then plunged within a few minutes, I'm not surprised that it didn't function normally."

Ellen was on the phone with NBC, checking to see if they had power.

"Okay, the show is about to resume," Ellen said, "but we probably lost most of our audience, or at least those without emergency generators."

Ellen, as well as the rest of us, gradually adjusted to the weather's surprises.

CHAPTER TWENTY SEVEN

"Hey Nance," Bill Cranston said. "If it weren't for your quick thinking, God knows what could have happened."

"Thanks for the compliment, hon, but something is scaring the shit out of me. That goddam fail-*safe* program is supposed to be just that—fail safe. I designed the software, and that's why I'm freaking out. What happened is not supposed to happen. It's impossible, but that's not accurate because the impossible just occurred. I also helped design series of switches that make up the override protocol. But it almost seems like somebody else is involved in operating the solar panels on the satellites."

"Could it be somebody in Billings playing around?" Cranston said.

"Nothing happens to the satellite controls in Billings without Frank Morgan or Phil Duncan knowing about it," Nancy said. "That's the way they designed the control system, and it's a great idea. It's sort of like the Black Box that travels around with the president. Nobody can launch a nuke without the president's input, and nobody can test the satellites without the express permission of Morgan or Duncan. You and I can't decide to do it on our own. The sequence must start in Billings. I don't expect that they'll run any more tests until we sort out this shit."

"*Stargazer* this is Rosetta, please come in," sounded the voice over the speaker.

"This is *Stargazer*, go ahead Rosetta," Cranston said.

"Bill, Nancy, this is Phil Duncan. Nancy, you helped us to avoid a disaster, God bless you. So now we're just faced with a mess, not a calamity. I feel kind of dumb to ask you this question, because I'm sure you two have discussed it, but do you have any idea what happened?"

"It's not a dumb question, Phil, and yes, we have been discussing it," Nancy said. "The simple answer is that neither of us has any idea what went wrong. As you well know, I was the design team head for both the fail-safe software and the override procedure. At least the override worked, thank God. But the malfunctioning fail-safe system is a mystery. I assume you still follow the standard practice where you or Frank Morgan enter numbers into the computer to okay a test."

"The protocol hasn't changed a bit, Nancy. Remember it was mandated by the Department of Defense. We've got all our engineers and scientist in brainstorming mode, and you can expect to hear from us from time to time with questions. As usual I will be the only one who communicates with you."

"What if somebody else from Billings calls us?" Nancy asked.

"That will mean that there's trouble, big trouble," Duncan said. "To channel all communications with *Stargazer* through one person, me, is yet another measure of security as you know. It hasn't changed. So, until you hear from me again, you two can get back to your Scrabble game, or whatever it is you do." Duncan stifled a laugh as he said that.

"So that means that you and I are free to figure out what to do with our time," Cranston said after Duncan signed off.

"Gimme a kiss, wiseass. Let's play Scrabble."

CHAPTER TWENTY EIGHT

"CIA Director Carlini is on the secure line for you, Mr. Secretary."
"Hello, Bill," I said. "I trust you're enjoying our summer weather."
"Very funny, Rick. It's freezing here in Langley, but at least the snow stopped falling. Meteorologists, for what they're worth, say that we're in for a few days of clear but freezing cold weather. I read your top secret briefing this morning about your conversation with Frank Morgan, the head man at the Rosetta Corporation. No sooner had I read it when I got a call from the White House."

"The White House called me too," I said. "For once I think they pulled their heads out of their asses and are starting to make some sense. I think the president has kicked some butt to get those jerkoffs to stop playing office games."
"I agree, Rick, they are beginning to make sense. They've stopped listening to the global warming 'experts,' especially since your charming wife made mincemeat out of that guy on her show the other day. They're starting to think what I'm thinking, and I'll bet you're thinking the same thing too."

"Yes, I think that all this shit may not be a natural phenomenon, but may be the result of intentional acts. I've checked up on the two astronauts who control the *Stargazer*. The commander, Nancy Mullin, is one hell of a sharp engineer. She thinks the weather events are linked to Rosetta's satellite tests. Mullin says that it's impossible, yet she recognized that it happened."

"I also hear that she's in the middle of a global warming style love affair with her fellow crewmember Bill Cranston," Carlini said.

"You CIA types love to get down to the smallest detail, don't you?"

"That's why they call us spooks, Rick. Last week one of them forgot to turn off the video monitor from Montana. Wow, quite a show. They really have fun with the weightless environment. I ordered the tape destroyed. No sense embarrassing people we need to rely on. But to change the subject, I want to know if Jake Arnold, the president's chief of staff, told you what he told me."

"Arnold told me the president wants to get deep inside," I said. "I flat out asked him if he could tell me what 'inside' means. All he said was Rosetta. I'm guessing the CIA is already inside."

"You're the only one I would say this to, Rick, but yes we are inside—deep inside. We've had a few key people there for months, long before this weather crap. Any company that launches 20 satellites with moveable solar panels needs to be watched. So far, nothing. What Morgan the CEO told you, Rick, is pretty much what we've come up with. The weather events appear to have been caused by malfunctioning solar panels, and by that I mean a malfunction of the fail-safe system. Our pretty astronaut friend, Nancy Mullin, was the chief designer of the system and she thinks it's impossible for the system to fail. But she admits that it did fail—big time. So, the White House wants us to get inside more so than we already are, which brings us back to your question—inside where?"

"That's what spooks are for, no?" I said.

"Yes, and with your permission I'd like to send a visitor your way."

"Let me guess," I said. "Buster?"

"The one and only, Mr. Super Spook himself. He's on assignment on another matter in New Jersey. He can be at your office within an hour."

I couldn't have been happier with that phone call. Buster, aka George Atkins, aka Gamal Akhbar, aka a ton of other aliases, is a true spy, and a brilliant one. He's tall and looks Middle Eastern, an appearance he inherited from his Coptic Christian Egyptian parents. He's fluent in Arabic and has the brassiest pair of balls imaginable. He's just the guy we need for this operation, whatever the hell this operation is.

"Sarah, it's Rick. I want you to come to my office. We're about to get a visit from our old friend Buster."

***

"Mr. Secretary, an Agent Atkins is here to see you. He says that you're expecting him." Sally Boynton, my assistant, knows Buster well, but, like the trained agent she is, you'd never know it because she'd never tell you.

Buster walked in, smiling broadly. With a warm, outgoing personality like his, you'd never suspect that he's a hard-nosed CIA agent.

"Mr. Secretary, Madam Director, a pleasure to see you folks again."

"You can make it Rick and Sarah, Buster," I said. "No need for formalities. We all know one another. Bill Carlini tells me you have some ideas to share with us."

"I do, Rick, and I'm not sure where I'm going with them yet, but I never do at the start of an investigation. As you know, my background is in science and engineering. I'm not the only techie to suspect that the bullshit we've been going through isn't a natural phenomenon. I've huddled with some very sharp scientists from NASA and we all concluded the same thing—that human actors are involved. Having said that, not one of us can explain how the solar panels on those satellites can be manipulated to bypass the fail-safe system."

"With all due respect, my friend," Sarah Watson said, "you're telling us that you've come to the same conclusion we have."

"It's a bit more nuanced than that, Sarah," Buster said. "Obviously we're talking about terror, and when we say terror, especially terror of a sophisticated quality, we suspect the Islamic State, ISIS. They haven't been quiet recently, as the recent attacks tell us. But there's a big difference between the recent ISIS operations and our current problem. ISIS has begun to launch actions all over the world, but the attacks are similar in one respect: they're simple. They use cars, trucks, knives, guns, and explosives, and train their sights on soft targets. Any psychopath could pull off the shit they've been engaging in lately. I think we're dealing with something we've never seen before, a highly sophisticated attack on something that's basic to all of us, the weather. If it *is* ISIS, and I have my doubts, they must be aligned with some people who are a hell of a lot more advanced than they are. To make sure we're all thinking in the right direction, let me ask you folks who you suspect."

"Have you ever watched my wife's show, *The Ellen Bellamy Show*?" I asked.

"Sure, it's my favorite show next to *Homeland*," Buster said. "If I can't watch it live, I DVR it. Your wife has a rare talent for getting people to talk. I've fantasized about hiring her to help me interrogate suspects."

"Then you've no doubt seen her interview climate change experts," I said. "I'm not sure when NBC will book the next one because those experts seem to be afraid of Ellen. Over coffee the other day she asked me if I thought these climate fanatics could have something to do with the weather. They have a vested interest in millions of dollars in grant money. If they can convince the world that climate change is the cause of these weather anomalies, the grant money spigots will open and flow. Hell, an article in today's *Wall Street Journal* talked about the sudden increase in foundation spending on climate change. It may sound conspiratorial, but it's a valid area of inquiry."

"What Rick just said makes a lot of sense, Buster. What do you think?" Sarah Watson said.

"Rick is one smart cookie, and I would never dismiss his thoughts on anything, but, as I just said, these weather events are terror. It would be out of character for these timid scientist types to collude and plunge the world into chaos. No, my money is on somebody else, somebody we haven't identified yet. Square one is obviously the Rosetta Corporation. As I said, I've got people inside, and I'm going to recommend that the FBI send in a team, not clandestinely like my guys, but as the investigators they are. I must humbly admit that FBI agents are fabulous interrogators. In a shootout, I'll pick my people, but the FBI people know how to ask the right questions without drawing a gun."

"Do you think you might find some of the people responsible right there at Rosetta?" Sarah asked.

"No, I don't, but if we did it would be a welcome gift. What I'm looking for are leads. That's the whole point of the operation at this stage. I recommend that all these efforts be channeled through Homeland Security to keep the CIA and FBI agents out of each other's hair. We've been working well together in the past few years, but there's got to be a coordinating command, and I suggest that Secretary Rick is the perfect man. Hey, the three of us know that there are leads out there—it always happens, and it will happen with this operation. Then we can nail those bastards—hopefully before the next blizzard."

CHAPTER TWENTY NINE

July 25

NYPD Officer Frank Monroe walked down Seventh Avenue in Manhattan on his regular foot patrol. He wore a pair of special nonskid shoes designed for walking on snow and ice. He didn't know if he would be reimbursed by the department, but he didn't care. He had spent enough time in the past few days falling on his ass, so he knew he had to do something about it. The temperature was 24 degrees on the bright July day. The temperature had warmed a bit yesterday, actually rising above freezing at one point. The slight thaw, combined with this morning's bright sun, worried Monroe. He could see chunks—*chunks*—of ice falling onto Seventh Avenue. He had just crossed 56th Street when he saw a man in front of him almost hit by a falling shard of heavy ice. Then he saw another sheet of ice hit the ground. He placed his whistle in his mouth and blew as hard as his lungs allowed.

"Everybody get inside a building," he yelled. "Get inside now, *RIGHT NOW.*"

Jeanine Fogarty, a clerk at the Midtown North Precinct, was a good friend Frank Monroe. They dated occasionally, but not as much as she would like. Jeannine was about to enter an office building on Monroe's command when she stopped, turned around, and yelled.

"Hey, Frank, what about *you*? Get your ass inside."

As Monroe smiled and waved at Jeannine, a huge chunk of ice landed on his head. Officer Frank Monroe was now an oozing red mass under a pile of crushed ice.

CHAPTER THIRTY

July 26

New York State Chief Administrative Judge Randolph Jackson sat in his office with Janet Pinkerton, his chief clerk.

"Janet, to say that this crap is getting out of control is to overstate the obvious. Under normal circumstances our courts are clogged with caseloads, but this weather is turning our judicial system into fucking chaos, pardon my language. Look at this report. All the lockups at all the courts in the state are at capacity. Some judges have ordered that old school buildings be taken over as temporary jails. The problem in New York City is at a crisis point. Rikers Island, which was crowded already before this weather hit, can't hold *one additional inmate*. The ACLU has taken notice and our courts are drowning under release petitions. Because jurors can't get to court, the dockets back up like a sewer. Jury trials are not considered an emergency, and that means the recent local law making it a felony to travel unless it's an emergency is bringing the system to a halt. The constitution gives a defendant a right to a speedy trial, but the constitution never contemplated non-stop blizzards in the summer."

"I just received an update from all districts this morning, your honor. It's even worse than you described. Prisoners are being released all over the state, and even some violent offender suspects are out on the street. Homeland Security Secretary Bellamy recently stated for the record that the only positive thing about this wild weather is that it keeps criminals off the street as well as the rest of us. Turns out he was being too optimistic. According to recent police reports, looting and burglaries are at an all-time high. And this insane weather only hit us 10 days ago."

"What about the civil calendars, Janet?"

"Frozen in amber, judge. If you have a contract you want enforced or a personal injury case that is ready for trial, you're out of luck. Some attorneys are waiving their client's right to a jury trial because you can't have a jury trial without a jury. Even if this crazy weather changes soon it will take years for us to work through the backlog. I've never seen anything like this, your honor."

"Do you have any statistics on the kind of cases that are being filed?"

"Yes, sir, and this blows me away. Although it's only been 10 days since the freeze and the blizzards started, we're seeing a 25 percent increase in bankruptcy filings. A lot of businesses are doing absolutely no business. I expect that in the weeks and months to come we'll see a lot more bankruptcies as suppliers go belly up. And we're just talking about New York. The same problems are hitting courts across the country. It's just a matter of time before we see how hard the economy as a whole is hit. And there's not a damn thing we can do about it other than to encourage plea bargains and civil settlements. We've got a problem, judge, a big one."

"I have a meeting with the governor this afternoon and I want you with me, Janet. I understand that we'll get picked up by a big snowmobile. You and I never expected this crap when we went to law school."

CHAPTER THIRTY ONE

"This is Cal Johnson reporting for *NBC News*. I'm here at the emergency room at Lenox Hill Hospital in Manhattan with Dr. Murray Goodman, as he's taking a well-earned break. Tell us, Dr. Goodman, what have you seen here at the emergency room as a result of our weather crisis?"

"I've never seen anything like what's going on here, Cal. With the freezing temperatures, I expected to see cases of frost bite and hyperthermia. We've had a few cases like that, of course, but what's clogging our emergency room are people with fractures—arms, wrists, legs, ankles, backs, necks, and skulls. It's as if the entire city decided to play tackle football—without pads. The culprit is obvious, as you folks have been saying on *The Ellen Bellamy Show*—black ice, the worst I've ever seen. But it's not only broken bones. We've seen at least 10 cases of people being injured by falling shards of ice. One person is in critical condition having had his arm severed. The rapid temperature swings are causing this. Snow and ice falling from tall buildings have always been a problem, but the rapid freeze-thaw turns those frozen sheets of ice into daggers when the temperature heats up a bit.

Ice in large blocks are also falling from building ledges. Yesterday a New York City policeman was killed by a chunk of ice that fell from a building. That happened right after a man in front of him was almost hit by a sheet of ice. I tell all our people here at the hospital to try to keep their outdoor walking to a minimum, and to walk through building when possible. I commend Ellen Bellamy for sounding the alarm loud and clear, but a lot of people haven't listened. When we encountered that weird heat spell, it lasted only two hours, but long enough to cause rivers of melting snow and sheets of falling ice, which quickly refroze when the temperatures dropped again. Please people, listen to me—be careful."

***

"Good afternoon everybody, and welcome to *The Ellen Bellamy Show*. You just saw a clip of NBC reporter Cal Johnson interviewing an emergency room doctor at Lenox Hill, where they're up to their eyeballs with fracture cases, the result of people falling on black ice, not to mention injuries caused by sheets of ice falling off buildings. The sudden thaw resulted in temperatures hitting the high 80s, and it lasted for a couple of hours, long enough to cause treacherous melting. It's easy to say don't leave home, but people must, if only to stock up on groceries and medicine. Many of the major footwear companies, including Nike, Jordan, and Adidas, sell models of shoes that include the name 'black ice,' which are designed for walking on, you guessed it, black ice. There are also traction devices that you can attach to your regular shoes. If you want to buy a pair of those shoes or traction devices, I suggest ordering online rather than going out to the store. Delivery people know how to walk on slippery surfaces, so leave it up to them. And avoid walking next to buildings when you can.

"My next guest is Professor James Tomkins from Columbia University, an expert in climate studies. He wrote the book, *The Truth about Climate Change – Don't Believe What You Have Heard*."

Sarah, Buster, and I were standing off to the side of the sound stage. Ellen was still broadcasting from my office.

"Professor Tomkins," Ellen said, "please give us your ideas on this severe weather, and what it has to do with climate change." Before he spoke

Ellen held up his book.

"Thank you for inviting me on your show, Ellen. Let me get right to my point. The unprecedented weather has nothing to do with climate change. Any opposite opinion is science fiction, not science. Climate change and global warming are serious phenomena, and it can't be denied that the earth is warming, and has warmed significantly in the past few years, partially from manmade causes. But this current weather anomaly is just that, an anomaly. Although I don't know what caused it, I do know that the culprit is *not* climate change, a process that occurs over decades and centuries. I've seen you interview some of my colleagues, and I commend you for your bluntness in attacking their theories, theories that are not only unproven but are totally unfounded. I would be happy to debate any of those alarmists on your show, but I think they're afraid of you."

"Doctor, do you think that this weather could be the result of intentional human action? In other words, could a human actor or actors cause these weird events?"

"Ellen, if you asked me that question before the weather calamity occurred I would have said that it's impossible. But the impossible has happened, so I'm not going to rule out an intentional act, which would amount to an act of terrorism—highly advanced terrorism. I wish I had a better answer for you and your viewers, but, unlike some of my colleagues, I'm not going to look for headlines by spouting nonsense."

I had asked Ellen to question this guy about the intentional act scenario. Leaking ideas can sometimes result in leads.

"Thank you, professor, for your excellent survey of a complex issue, and for letting in some fresh air on a lot of nonsense. I hope to have you on the show in the future as we learn more about this phenomenon. This is Ellen Bellamy, thanking you folks for joining us today. So, stay warm, stay safe, and stay tuned to NBC for the latest news."

Sarah, Buster, and I walked over to the set as they were taking off the sound equipment. Ellen introduced us to Tomkins.

"I hope I'm not under arrest," he said with a laugh.

"It's a pleasure to see Ellen interview somebody who isn't full of shit,"

Sarah Watson said. "I just downloaded your book onto my Kindle."

"I've read a lot about you Doctor Tomkins," I said. "It's no secret that the government is taking a great interest in this weather, and not just from a safety point of view. I heard what you said about the possibility of an intentional act, and I'd like you to consider joining my staff as a consultant. I've got the budget for it, and I know that you have a top-secret security clearance. If there is an active player in this calamity, it's our topmost priority to find out who it is and to put a stop to it. If somebody or some group has figured out a way to change the weather, it makes all other terrorist activities, including the threat of nuclear weapons, small stuff. The three of us, Buster, Sarah, and I, represent the muscle. We need brains like yours."

"Speaking of brains, don't overlook your lovely wife here," Tomkins said. "Yes, I'd be happy to help out in any way I can."

"Thank you for the compliment, professor," Ellen said. "I agree with Director Watson. It was a pleasure to interview a climate scientist who isn't full of shit."

CHAPTER THIRTY TWO

"NASA Flight 17, NASA Flight 17, this is NASA Headquarters, come in please."

NASA Flight 17 was a DC-8 aircraft designed to track weather systems, usually hurricanes.

"This is Major Carl Hofmeister on Flight 17, go ahead, NASA."

"Anything new to report, Carl? This is Jim Loudon, duty officer at headquarters."

"Absolutely nothing new, Jim. Since that sudden rapid thaw and refreeze last week I expected we'd see some atmospheric changes, but we haven't. Since the snow stopped, the view is beautiful, if you can call a snowy landscape in July beautiful. This plane is designed to get the shit kicked out of it and keep flying, but we could be flying a Piper Cub. No turbulence at all. The outside temperature is minus 10, but we're at 20,000 feet. Our nearest weather station on the ground in South Dakota shows a temperature of 19 degrees, nothing by South Dakota standards, but cold as hell for the summertime."

"How's your copilot Marty doing?"

"This is Lt. Marty Baxter speaking. As the major indicated, we're having an unmemorable flight."

"Hey, congratulations, Marty" Loudon said. "I understand your wife had a baby boy last week."

"Thanks, Jim. Debbie is looking forward to taking the baby outside but it's too cold."

A bright light enshrouded the cockpit. The plane suddenly lurched upward, and then dove, nose down, levelling off at 15,000 feet, 5,000 feet lower than their cruising altitude.

"What the fuck was that?" Major Hofmeister yelled. "It felt like we were hit by a truck."

Beep, beep, beep sounded the emergency alarm.

"Oh my God, the instruments show that we've lost hydraulics," Lt. Baxter yelled.

"We're losing altitude, NASA," Hofmeister shouted, "and without hydraulics I've lost control of the aircraft. We're going down, NASA."

"Talk to me Carl," Louden said. "What's happening?"

"Before we dove, we were surrounded by the brightest light I've ever seen," Hofmeister said, his voice cracking. "It looked like a…"

"Come in Flight 17, come in Flight 17. What's going on Carl?"

The last thing that the ground control crew heard was a loud static noise, possibly indicating an explosion.

CHAPTER THIRTY THREE

July 27

"Al Roker here for *NBC Weather*, folks. Well, we're in yet another temperature reversal. The temperature here in Manhattan is a perfect 79 degrees, normal for the July 27. So I guess you expect me to give you a happy-face report. I'd like to, but I can't. I'm worried about something, and so are the folks at NOAA. What we see as a reprieve from the bizarre temperature plunge, is not something to be happy about, not in the short term anyway. The conditions, with warm temperatures at ground level, and freezing temperatures above create a perfect condition for tornados. According to the reading from our weather balloon this morning, the overhead freezing temperatures are close to us, not what you would expect from a normal summer weather pattern. I have on the line Jerome Williamson, a tornado expert from NOAA, who will bring us up to date on what we may expect."

"Good morning, Al, and thanks for having me on your show. What you said about the conditions for tornadic activity are true. Instability in the atmosphere—and God knows we've had a lot of that recently, combined with the powerful downdrafts or wind shear make us wary of what may happen.

"The Fujita Scale, used to determine the strength of a tornado, is like the Saffir-Simpson scale for measuring hurricane strength. The most extreme tornado was the Tri-State Tornado which touched down in parts of Missouri, Illinois, and Indiana in 1929. Although the scale wasn't in existence at the time, scientists determined that the tornado had a strength of F5, the largest ever. Another F5 tornado was the Bridge Creek-Moore Tornado that hit Oklahoma in 1999. It clocked wind speeds of over 301 mph."

"Mr. Williamson, what can you tell our viewers about how they can minimize the threat of a tornado?" Roker said.

"Once a tornado hits and you're in the middle of it, the only thing you can do is pray. But there are two watchwords we always think about with tornados: vigilance and preparedness. If a tornado is heading your way, it's too late to *think* how to get away. You should run for a below-ground shelter, such as a basement or a subway. Stay away from windows and keep your outdoor surroundings clear of objects that can turn into fast moving projectiles."

"Do you see a possibility of a tornado hitting New York City, Mr. Williamson?"

"Tornados have hit New York, but the consequences were downed trees and damage caused by flying debris, nothing like the devastating twisters that have hit the Midwest."

"Thank you for visiting with us," Roker said. "I'm not sure I feel safer after listening to Mr. Williamson, but I do feel more prepared. Well, folks, be vigilant and be prepared to act. Al Roker, signing off from *NBC News.*"

CHAPTER THIRTY FOUR

The living quarters on *Stargazer* were suddenly bathed in an all-pervasive brightness.

"What the hell's going on," Nancy Mullin yelled, as she put her hand over her eyes. "I've never seen anything so bright."

"Let's check on the satellite solar panels to make sure one didn't accidently deploy while facing us," Bill Cranston said.

"Rosetta headquarters, Rosetta headquarters, this is Nancy Mullin on *Stargazer*."

"This is Rosetta. Please hold, Nancy, while I get Phil Duncan," said the radio operator. Strict orders were for Phil Duncan, and only Phil Duncan, to communicate with the crew of *Stargazer*.

"Go ahead, Nancy, this is Phil Duncan."

"We've just been hit by the brightest light we've ever seen," Nancy said. "Bill checked the solar panels on the satellites and nothing's deployed, thank God. Wait a minute, Bill is showing me a video replay of earth a couple of minutes ago. Jesus, we need to wear sunglasses to look at it. There was an extremely bright light on the ground, which also covered a hell of a lot of sky, emanating from the western United States. It looked like it was around the Dakotas. The light started as a flash but then persisted for about a minute. We're going to check of all our instruments to make sure nothing's been compromised."

"I'm starting with the satellite monitoring systems," Cranston said. "Video feed, check; main panel power, check; fail-safe system down, but we already knew that; solar panel override switch, DOWN. Holy shit, we don't dare run another solar panel test with the override down. Now I'm checking the onboard environmental systems. Main panel, check; lighting systems, check; video feeds, check; atmospheric control—DOWN. He looked at Nancy as she wiped perspiration off her forehead. It's getting hot in here, Phil. I'm going to dress for a spacewalk to see if I can fix the atmospheric controller."

Nancy Mullin helped Cranston into his space suit. Before she put his helmet on she leaned over to his ear.

"Be careful, baby. If you see something you don't understand, don't touch it."

Cranston eased himself through the hatch leading to the airlock that opened into space. He floated up to the instrument panel on the outside of *Stargazer* and, after checking it for static electricity, removed the cover. His hunch proved correct—a burned out solenoid, possibly damaged by the gigantic flash of light. He replaced it and spoke to Nancy over the radio. "Flick the console on, Nance."

"Perfect, Bill, you're a genius. Now we'll be able to play Scrabble later in comfort."

Phil Duncan, who was listening in, laughed.

"While I'm out here, I'm going to check the transmitter on the satellite override switch."

He moved himself 10 feet to the left and located the override switch cover. He opened it, expecting to find another malfunctioning solenoid. The solenoid was not damaged.

"Phil, if you're listening, I expected to find a burned-out solenoid on the override switch. It's in perfect shape. But having said that, what the hell could be causing the override problem? Dare we test the solar panels without knowing what the problem is?"

"No, Bill, we can't take that chance," Duncan said. "Great work, pal. Now get back inside or you'll be late for your Scrabble game."

CHAPTER THIRTY FIVE

July 28

"Good afternoon everyone, Martha McCallum reporting for *Fox News*. Unfortunately, I have a tragedy to report. NASA Flight 17, a DC-8 plane that was used to track weather, especially major storms like hurricanes, has crashed in South Dakota. We have heard a report from the NTSB that the plane experienced an extreme flash of intense light from the ground, and it lasted for about a minute. The plane lost all hydraulic controls, which made it almost impossible to fly. It's unclear whether the flash of light had anything to do with the crash, but the loss of hydraulics came moments after the sudden light and therefore it's under suspicion. I'm sad to report that the pilot and co-pilot lost their lives.

"In other news, the weather of course. The Department of Homeland Security has announced that it's exploring every possible scenario that could have resulted in our insane weather. Richard Bellamy, Secretary of Homeland Security is on the line to bring us up to date."

"Good afternoon, Mr. Secretary. I hope you're going to tell us not to put our summer clothes away on this July day, not yet anyway. Please tell us what's new."

"Hello, Martha, and hello to your viewers. I wish I could give you more definitive news, but let me just say that the weather is now *the* major priority on the federal government's list of urgent matters. We're treating this weather as we would a war. Nothing is off the table, and we've assembled a team of scientists and engineers to help us."

"Is there any truth to the rumor that the government thinks this event could have been intentional, in other words man-made?"

"As I said, Martha, nothing is off the table and we're exploring every avenue. I know it sounds incredible that this weather could have been the result of a deliberate act, but let's face it, the entire event is incredible."

"Thank you for taking the time to talk to us, Mr. Secretary."

"In other news…"

CHAPTER THIRTY SIX

July 28

"Good morning everyone, Darryl Smith for *NBC News*. We've received word from the Office of Emergency Management and from the New York City mayor's office, that major snow clearing has begun on this beautiful but still freezing July 28th. The emergency local law against driving unless you have permission from the Office of Emergency Management is still in effect. Because the temperatures remain below freezing, despite the two-hour thaw a couple of days ago, the plows have a hard time finding places to drop the snow. Sanitation trucks and private construction vehicles have been enlisted to carry snow to the East and Hudson Rivers and drop it in the water.

"I'm happy to announce that our own Ellen Bellamy will be returning to our studio after broadcasting her show from the Federal Office Building for the past few days. Ellen's husband, as you know, is Rick Bellamy, the Secretary of Homeland Security, and was gracious enough to enable NBC to broadcast her show from his government office. Just so you know, NBC paid the going rate for the privilege of broadcasting from federal property. We tried to cut a deal, but Ellen's husband is a tough negotiator.

"I close this segment with a question we all have. What else can go wrong?"

CHAPTER THIRTY SEVEN

July 30

"This is fucking impossible," Admiral John Campbell said to Captain Frank Paluzzo, commanding officer of the *USS Gerald R. Ford*, flagship of Carrier Strike Group 2600. Campbell was the commanding officer of the strike group. The *Ford*, along with a cruiser and two frigates, steamed across the Pacific for the Sea of Japan, where it would rendezvous with ships of the Japanese and South Korean navies for maneuvers. The purpose of the exercises was to try to convince Kim Jong-un, the boy dictator of North Korea, to pull back on his provocations and nuclear ambitions.

"Do you think that fat kid in North Korea could have something to do with this?" Admiral Campbell asked. "Our previous fix as of a couple of minutes ago showed us 1,200 miles southeast of Japan. Now our satellites show us off the coast of Bermuda. What about our other systems, Frank?"

"Our inertial navigation system shows us where we know we are, 1,200 miles southeast of Japan," Captain Paluzzo said. "This is one for the books, admiral. I'm wondering if our cold temperature could have something to do with this. I don't have a clue why this happened. Satellites are satellites, and they're not programmed to play games. They either work or not, but they never put out wrong positions. I recommend that we contact Norfolk, sir."

The huge United States Navy base at Norfolk, Virginia was the home-port of the *USS Gerald R. Ford* and the accompanying ships in her strike group. Like all other areas of the country, Norfolk was blanketed in snow. The lines from the ships to the piers were festooned with hanging icicles.

"This is Naval Station Norfolk, Lieutenant James Stockton speaking. Read you loud and clear, captain. If you're calling to report a problem with your satellite navigation, sir, let me tell you that we've assigned 10 extra officers on radio and phone duty to answer calls from the fleet. I've been instructed to tell you to rely on your inertial navigation, and to get a celestial fix tonight if possible."

***

"Garmin, Limited, Marilyn Freund speaking, may I help you."

"This is Steve Bowden, Operations VP of General Motors, may I please speak to your CEO."

"Jim Blackwell here, go ahead, Steve, although I think I already know what you're calling about."

"You mean my cars aren't the only ones with GPS problems? What the hell is going on, Jim?"

"When my best customer asks me what's going on, I want to give him a straight answer," Blackwell said, "but you won't be happy with my response, which is that I haven't got a fucking hint, nor do any of my people. I personally called the Rosetta Corporation, the company whose satellites we've used for the past year because they're so reliable. They have no idea what's wrong. I also called the heads of the other top five GPS manufacturers. They've been having the same problem as us. For the time being, Steve, we're all back to the good old days of pulling into a gas station to get directions."

"Mr. Blackwell, there's an emergency call from the Secretary of Homeland Security on the line two," his assistant said.

"Gotta go, Steve. Homeland Security is calling. As you know, we have a lot of government contracts. I'll call you when I have something to tell you."

"This is Jim Blackwell for Garmin, Mr. Secretary. In answer to the question I know you're about to ask, we've lost all satellite communication in all our units, whether shipboard, vehicular, or handheld."

"Have you been in touch with the other manufacturers, Jim?"

"Yes, sir, and they all report the same thing. Our GPS units simply aren't working. I called Rosetta Corporation, the outfit that controls most of the satellites, and they claim they're in the dark as much as we are. How's the military doing, sir, especially the Navy?"

"Because you have a top-secret clearance and a need to know, I'll give you the bad news," Bellamy said. "Naval Operations reports that all ships at sea have lost satellite navigation. Garmin isn't our only contractor. All the other GPS providers are down too. I think it's obvious that the problem isn't with your units or anyone else's. The problem seems to be with the satellites themselves—or the satellite manufacturer."

***

"The goddam thing says to stay on the current road for three more miles," the man said to his wife, feeling angry because she wanted him to stop at a service station for directions.

They were heading toward a luxury condominium complex in South Carolina where they would vacation for a week at a traded time-share unit. The roads were hilly and there seemed to be a curve every few hundred feet.

"Honey, look at the map on the dashboard," his wife said. "The friggin GPS doesn't seem to know what road we're on. It says Palmer Drive, but I haven't seen any road signs with that name on it. We just passed a sign that says we're on Higgins Lane. Hey, slow down."

The man's frustration was filtering through to his right foot. They went around a long curve doing 62 miles per hour. As soon as the road straightened, they could see a hedgerow directly in front of them. Unable to slow down on the sudden sheet of ice, the car went through the hedge and careened off a cliff, diving 100 feet to the rocky coastline below.

The local radio station reported the fifth single-car crash that day, all of which resulted in fatalities.

Chapter 38

"I have the report you asked for, Bartholomew," his assistant, Douglas Merriman, said.

"Read it to me Douglas. Would you care for a cup of coffee?"

"No, thank you, Bartholomew."

Bartholomew Martin insisted that all his subordinates call him by his first name, as he called all of them. Occasionally someone would slip and call him "Mr. President," which would always result in a cold stare from Bartholomew, and occasionally a brief chastisement. Bartholomew Martin was the 46th President of the United States, defeated in a landslide election two years ago by Matthew Blake. Now, instead of a country, Martin leads a group called *The Reformers*.

The men sat in Martin's large den, overlooking a fruit tree garden on his compound in Erbil, Kurdistan.

"Both of the two recent tests of the Rosetta satellites," the report began, "resulted in the weather anomalies that we have experienced. Our solar array field in South Dakota became operational two days ago and resulted in the crash of a weather tracking plane."

Bartholomew waved his hand.

"Enough minutia that I already know about," Bartholomew said. "When does the report say that the final transfer will take place?"

Merriman flipped through the pages of the report.

"The present schedule calls for the final transfer in two weeks,"

"That will be all," Bartholomew said.

He walked from his den out onto the wooden deck. The house was large at 8,000 square feet, far bigger than the typical house in Kurdistan. Bartholomew designed it himself and retained a major architectural firm in Italy to draw up the building plans. He lived there alone, his wife having died a few years before in a mysterious car accident that was never explained. A sudden wind blew across the large deck, making the air frigid at 25 degrees Fahrenheit, the kind of weather that Bartholomew loves. The normal temperature in Kurdistan in July is between 90 and 100 degrees Fahrenheit, which meant that Bartholomew always stayed inside the perfectly climate-controlled house in the summer. What everyone was calling "the weather anomaly" took its toll on the Middle East as well. Although it could be cold in the winter, the temperature seldom fell below freezing. Nevertheless, Bartholomew installed a heating system to ward off the winter chill. One never knows when the temperature may take a sudden dive, he thought. One of the wealthiest men in the world, Bartholomew seldom spared himself the best in creature comforts.

He bent over and lit a cigar, his back turned against the wind, and looked over his property. The world thought it could forget Bartholomew Martin, he pondered, laughing out loud.

CHAPTER THIRTY NINE

July 31

Mitchel Langdon, an expert on satellite navigation, better known as GPS or Global Positioning System, was a guest on *The Ellen Bellamy Show*.

"It's hard to imagine," Ellen said, "but GPS devices have been in cars for over 20 years, the first ones installed in 1995. Since then we've learned to take them for granted. No more pulling over to the side of the road to consult a paper map or pulling into a filling station to ask someone directions. The voice in the dashboard tells you when to turn and how far it is to your destination. If you're like me, your sense of direction is shot to pieces because we rely so much on the voice of the lady in the dashboard, the GPS. But suddenly we're back to paper maps and the guy in the gas station. As of yesterday afternoon, the Global Positioning System is not functioning anywhere. According to the Navy, Coast Guard, and cruise line companies, satellite navigation at sea is nonexistent. Mr. Langdon, you're known as one of the world's leading experts on satellite navigation. You even helped create the technology decades ago. What's your take on this strange phenomenon?"

"Ellen, it's true that people turn to me with satellite navigation questions, but for once I don't have any answers. Instrumentation in the space station *Stargazer* shows that the satellites are all in place, but they're simply not receiving or sending data. They're just hunks of metal in orbit. The problem isn't just one of inconvenience. All of us could get around without satellites a few years ago, but because people have learned to rely on them, there have been numerous serious car accidents caused by people not knowing where they were. Young drivers don't even know how to unfold a paper map."

"Mr. Langdon, do you suspect that the satellite navigation problem could have something to do with our bizarre weather?"

"Because these incidents happened so close in time to each other, we have to suspect a connection. But as of now it's merely a correlation, not a causation. I don't know how a satellite problem could cause a severe drop in temperatures, and neither do my colleagues. We have our suspicions, but as of now it's a complete mystery."

"Thank you for joining us today Mr. Mitchell, and I hope we'll be seeing you again."

"Our next guest is one of the key leaders of our nation's military, Admiral Gregory Collins, Chief of Naval Operations. Because we don't have a satellite feed, you may notice the picture isn't clear from time to time. Admiral Collins, please tell us about satellite navigation in the Navy."

"As you probably know, Ellen, the Navy has been using satellite navigation a lot longer than civilians have been using it in their cars. We do have an advantage in that we never relied exclusively on satellites to take a position. We take what's called a celestial fix, which determines a position by the ship's location in relation to plotted stars. We also have sophisticated inertial navigation systems in our ships. But, like everybody, we've grown to rely on the simplicity of satellite navigation."

"We've grown to rely on a lot of things, admiral, including normal weather."

"True, Ellen. In the past few days we've been introduced to a new world."

CHAPTER FORTY

July 31

"*Stargazer, Stargazer*, this is Rosetta, come in."

"I've repeated that 10 times, Frank," Phil Duncan said to Rosetta CEO Frank Morgan. "Bottom line is that we're out of communication with *Stargazer*. Our primary communication was through satellite, so it shouldn't surprise us if we have trouble, but this is different. We're in a total blackout."

"Mr. Morgan, it's Homeland Security Secretary Bellamy on line one for you," his assistant said.

"I was about to call you, Mr. Secretary. Since I spoke to you a few hours ago we haven't been able to communicate with one satellite, not one. But it gets worse. Our space station *Stargazer* is off the grid as well. *Stargazer* is our link to the satellites. Without her, we're blind."

"Frank, I have with me a Mr. Atkins. He's a government investigator (Bellamy would never disclose that Buster is a CIA agent) and he's got a few questions. Is Phil Duncan with you?"

"Yes, Phil's here. Go ahead, Mr. Atkins, how can we help you?" Morgan said.

"At the time the satellites went down, a weather tracking airplane encountered an extremely bright flash from the ground in South Dakota," Buster said. "The aircraft lost its hydraulics and crashed."

"Yes," Morgan said. "I heard about that on the news. Because it was so close in time to the satellite blackout, we're following that as a lead, but it hasn't taken us anywhere."

Phil Duncan tugged on his shirtsleeve and pointed to the TV.

"Mr. Atkins, there's something coming in on the TV. I'm looking at *Fox News*."

"Good afternoon, ladies and gentlemen, Shepard Smith here for *Fox News*. We've just received a disturbing report of yet another plane crash, this time involving six aircraft. A squadron of Navy F/A-18 Hornet jets was flying in formation over New Jersey on their way to land on the *USS Abraham Lincoln*, an aircraft carrier steaming off the East Coast. The report said an enormous flash of bright light emanated from the ground in Southern New Jersey, near Cape May. One of the pilots managed to say that he had lost all control of the jet and it was nosing down. Fortunately, the planes were high enough to make for successful ejections. We've been told that all six pilots parachuted safely into the ocean and were picked up by motor launches. We will bring you further reports as they come in.

"In other news, there has been no official explanation for our loss of satellite communications this morning. All land vehicles, airplanes, and ships at sea are without satellite navigation. Not one GPS is working. Over the years we've gotten used to GPS as a matter of convenience and we were shocked when the government just announced that it's a national emergency. We forget that our satellite system is a vital part of our national security, not just the convenience of giving us directions in our cars. The military is treating this event as a direct attack on the country."

CHAPTER FORTY ONE

August 1

After today's show, Ellen joined me at 26 Federal Plaza. Although our house in Greenwich Village was not far, the state of our emergency screamed out for me to be on location and ready to respond to the changing situation.

We were in a moderating temperature pattern once again, but this time it was different. The temperature was going up, but more slowly than in the recent days. The thermometer read 60 degrees at At 6 p.m. as we stood by the window looking out at the snow-covered Manhattan streets. I don't know why we looked out the window so much. Were we expecting something different? We sipped cocktails before dinner. I've limited myself to one drink before dinner because I never knew when I would have to snap to and make fast decisions. Truth was, I felt like drinking a whole bottle of Scotch.

"Hey, Rick, it's getting dark as hell," Ellen said. "It can't be another snowstorm coming. It's too warm."

Writers love to use the word ominous. The word conveys the thought that some bad shit is about to happen. That friggin cloud looked *ominous*.

"Oh my God, look at that," Ellen said, pointing south over lower Manhattan. "That's a funnel cloud, a tornado."

I ran to my desk and pulled out a pair of binoculars. Having grown up and spent all my life in New York City, I had never seen a tornado, only in photos and on film. The gigantic cloud looked to be 10 blocks wide. The roaring sound was like a speeding train on our roof.

It wasn't just a tornado, but a gigantic tornado.

I handed the binoculars to Ellen. She turned the dial on the view finder to get a better closeup.

"Oh, no. I can't be seeing that. What's that debris I see flying? Tell me it's impossible."

I looked again through the binoculars. The debris that Ellen mentioned was vehicles—cars, busses, and trucks. The slushy but still deep snow began to swirl in front of us. Something pelted the window.

"Hey, let's go into the den. We shouldn't be near any windows."

A TV monitor in the den picked up the view outside 26 Federal Plaza from the security cameras pointed at the entrance. I breathed a cautious sigh of relief. The scene in front of the building was a riot of slush and rain, but it was not a tornado. I ran back to the window. The gigantic tornado moved off to the west. We dodged a bullet. After 15 minutes, the wind died, but we could still hear a distant roar and crashing sounds of flying debris, including vehicles. The tornado moved northwest up the Hudson River and, as we later discovered, would devastate Weehawken, New Jersey.

We looked at each other, speechless. Thankfully the window held. I looked down at the scene in front of 26 Federal Plaza. The twister obviously didn't come north to us, but a lot of debris did.

I tried the phone. Dead. Then my cell phone. Dead.

"Let's see if TV works," I said.

The strong TV infrastructure that the network execs put in place worked. Al Roker, his handsome dark face almost ashen white, was manning the microphone.

"Someday a playwright, an opera producer, or a novelist will summarize what just happened to lower Manhattan today. I'll try to fill you in on this devastation. Battery Park is a wasteland but thank God the twister didn't do much damage to the residential buildings in Battery Park City. Weehawken, New Jersey took the full brunt of the tornado, which picked up strength as it traveled up the Hudson River. We'll be updating you all day on the wreckage left in the path of the storm. According to the scientists at NOAA, the tornado clocked in on the Fujita Scale at a powerful F4. The strongest tornado ever that ever hit, registered F5 on the scale, so the lower Manhattan twister was a big one."

As Ellen and I watched the reports on TV, I wondered what was coming our way next.

CHAPTER FORTY TWO

August 2

"I've gotten so used to being near you, Bill, I hate the thought of being without you."

"I love being near you too, Nance, but I'd feel a little safer if we had communication with Rosetta. We're due for a resupply visit next week. They always call to alert us when the supply capsule is approaching. I have no idea how they're going to pull it off without communications."

"We'll just have to keep looking at the space around us to see if a supply pod is heading our way," Nancy said. "Once the capsule gets close, we can use shortwave radio. Until then, we're blind—and deaf."

"We took an inventory just two days ago, Nance. After about another three weeks we'll be down to water and saltine crackers, and precious few saltines at that. For now, we're going to work on a big assumption—that our only problem is communication. We have no idea if there's a technical issue in our connection to Montana."

"We can't even run tests without Montana knowing about it, Bill. Too dangerous. The only thing we have is each other—which is the most important thing."

"Hey, I've got a little surprise for you, Nance."

He handed her a small metal box with a string around it to serve as a bow.

"For me?"

"Who else? Open it."

She removed the string and opened the box. Inside was a ring made of aluminum. Bill had salvaged it from a toolbox.

"Marry me, hon. Make me the happiest man in space."

Nancy gave herself a shove off the bulkhead and did a 360-degree twirl. She then wrapped her arms around him and squeezed.

"The answer is yes! We may be low on supplies but now we have other things to do. Let's decide on a date and prepare the guest list. Once we have everything in place, reality may cooperate with us. I think we should celebrate."

"We don't have any wine or booze, Nance, so we'll have to come up with something else."

"We'll think of something."

CHAPTER FORTY THREE

"This is Phil Duncan with the Rosetta Corporation. May I speak to Secretary Bellamy, please?"

"Go ahead, Phil. I guess you heard about that huge tornado that wrecked a lot of lower Manhattan and New Jersey. I hope you have some better news than the last time we spoke."

"We're still in a communication blackout with *Stargazer*, Rick, and we're due to send a supply capsule next week. The astronauts are getting low on essentials, like food. Normally, we communicate with them days before the resupply flight so they can prepare for dockage, but now we can't. Our only choice is to launch the supply pod and hope they're looking for it."

"Any idea if you'll be able to communicate with the supply pod, Phil?"

"We just don't know, Mr. Secretary. If our communication blackout is the result of atmospheric or electrical conditions in space, the answer is no. Once the supply pod gets close to *Stargazer*, they can communicate with shortwave radio. We'll just have to launch the supply pod and hope for the best."

"What if you can't resupply the *Stargazer*, Phil?"

"To be blunt, our astronaut friends will starve to death within a month."

***

"It's the White House for you on line one, Mr. Secretary."

"Yes, Mr. President, Rick Bellamy here." Whenever I got a call from the White House I assumed it was President Blake on the line. He always likes to make his own calls, especially to old friends.

"Rick, I don't have to tell you how critical our linkup with the space station *Stargazer* is. We're getting full cooperation from the Rosetta Corporation, but that's not enough. From your recent reports, it seems that Rosetta no longer controls *Stargazer*. We're convinced that the tests they ran on the satellites resulted in the wild weather. We're satisfied that Rosetta had nothing directly to do with the event, but we don't know who *is* in control. The latest we've learned is that Rosetta not only has lost control of the station, but all communication links as well. This is deep shit, Rick. Bring me up to date on what you know."

"Mr. President, I share your concerns about the space station. We just found out about the communications blackout, but we also discovered another critical issue. *Stargazer* will run out of supplies in a week. Unless they're able to replenish from a supply ship, the two astronauts are as good as dead within a month. Rosetta tells me that they're going to attempt a resupply mission, but without communication with the station it could be risky. We hope that they'll be able to use shortwave radio. Everybody in government, including us at Homeland Security, has concluded that someone or some group is pulling this crap off. Whoever they are will soon be in total control of earth's weather, if they aren't already. As you know, sir, the temperatures have been moderating across the globe. We would normally greet that as good news, but, because we don't know who's in control, we can't sit back and relax. Ellen and I watched part of lower Manhattan get torn up by a tornado. Every scientist I talk to thinks the tornado had a lot to do with the weather anomalies."

"Rick, I know that Homeland Security is on top of this case. That's why I appointed you Secretary. Give me your latest thinking about suspects."

"Sir, we've been monitoring all those who we might call the usual suspects, people we know are not on our side: North Korea, Iran, Russia, and even China. As you know, we have spies deeply imbedded in all those countries. North Korea is a big problem because secrecy is a national sport. But we haven't seen a hint that Kim Jong-un has anything to do with the weather events. As of right now we have absolutely no idea who may be tampering with the climate. Rosetta Corporation has told us about the changes in satellite configurations, but even Rosetta doesn't know how it's being done, or who's doing it. Until we find out, we're at the mercy of whoever *is* in control. The critical issue right now is the resupply effort for the space station. If Rosetta can't pull it off, the two astronauts will die a nasty death and will leave the entire world at the mercy of some unknown force. Rosetta tells us that the resupply rocket is set to launch next Thursday, five days from now. Between then and now, there's nothing we can do but wait."

"Keep me updated on any changes, Rick. Please give my best to your lovely wife. As busy as I am I never miss *The Ellen Bellamy Show*, even though I may see it as a rerun at 2 a.m. Often I get better information from Ellen's show than I do from my security briefings."

CHAPTER FORTY FOUR

August 4

"Welcome to our show, ladies and gentlemen. I'm your host, Ellen Bellamy. Today we're going to talk about, what else, the weather. This morning, Al Roker gave us all an update on what's going on in the world of weather forecasting. I'm delighted that Al is our first guest this afternoon. Al, please tell us what's going on 'in your neck of the woods,' as you love to say."

"Ellen, this morning I spoke from the heart as well as from the mind. I talked about the change in weather forecasting, and the most dramatic change is this—traditional forecasting is out the window. Never in my life did I ever expect to see a tornado pop up suddenly—in Manhattan of all places. All we've been able to do, and all we can do, is report on what's happening now, or a short time from now based on radar. It's no government secret that we've lost communications with the space station *Stargazer* as of yesterday. We know that the recent bizarre weather changes had something to do with the 20 satellites that *Stargazer* controls. But now the Rosetta

Corporation, the company that owns and controls *Stargazer,* has not only lost control, but has lost communication. What we know now is somewhat good news. The temperatures have moderated worldwide and are approaching what is normal for early August. Right now, the thermometer reads 65 degrees, still chilly for August 4th, but it's gradually rising. The normal high for today in New York City is 82 degrees. If we pass that number, we may find ourselves as we did a few days ago in a sudden heat wave. So, we're keeping our fingers crossed, something I thought I'd never say as a meteorologist. Because we've lost all satellite communication, as I said this morning, besides short-term help from radar, my two favorite weather forecasting tools are my window and my telephone."

"Al, we've gotten reports that the *Stargazer* was due for a resupply mission next week. Can you tell us anything about the status of the two astronauts aboard?"

"Studies tell us that, with proper hydration, a human being can live for as long as about 40 days without food," Roker said. "I had the wonderful experience of visiting an orbital platform—*The International Space Station*—a couple of years ago. I can tell you that, even without gravity, your body still acts like it always did—you need to feed it. Docking a space capsule, such as a resupply pod, is every bit as complicated at it seems. Without communications between the resupply vehicle and *Stargazer,* the operation becomes a lot trickier. They'll have to talk via shortwave radio when the supply pod gets close enough. Our prayers are with Nancy Mullin and Bill Cranston, the two *Stargazer* astronauts."

"Thanks Al, for your usual expert opinion on a complex subject. Our next guest is retired four-star Air Force General, Philip Benton. General Benton, do you think some bad actors are involved in this crisis, or is it just a freak of nature?"

"Good afternoon, Ellen. In my opinion, there is nothing about the recent weather changes that is the result of chance. I believe that someone or some group is behind it. The activities are simply too complicated to be happenstance. I have no idea who may be involved, but I'm not on active duty so I wouldn't have security clearance or the need to know. But logic tells me that somebody is doing things to our weather."

"Thank you, General, and thank you all for joining us this afternoon. Don't miss tomorrow's show, everybody. We're going to take a closer look at who or what may be involved in our weather situation."

CHAPTER FORTY FIVE

August 5

The temperature in Erbil, the capital of Iraqi Kurdistan, had moderated as it had all over the world. The temperature was 74 degrees and it was raining heavily. Bartholomew Martin loved the rain, He stood puffing on a cigar on his deck under the overhead and watched the rain wash away the piles of snow.

"I have an update about the status of *Stargazer*, Bartholomew," Douglas Merriman said, as he shook the water from his umbrella. "Not only have they lost communication with Rosetta Corporation in Montana, but they have no communication linkup at all. *Stargazer* is on its own."

"So it's going as planned?"

"Yes, Bartholomew."

"What about next week's resupply mission, Douglas?"

"Our insider tells us that Rosetta is going forward with the resupply attempt, even though it will be risky. They're hoping that the crew of the *Stargazer* will see the approaching supply pod and adjust accordingly. The launch is set for Thursday."

"Sabotage the launch, Douglass. I don't know how, and I don't want any excuses. Make sure that rocket never leaves earth, or if it does, it explodes shortly thereafter. We will launch our own resupply mission from the company that manufactures our rockets in California, the same company that makes Rosetta's rockets."

***

Rosetta Corporation employs a reusable rocket system to bring back a part of the launch rocket for use in the next mission. The first successful recovery was in 2015 and the first successful relaunch occurred in March 2017. The company uses SpaceX's Dragon cargo craft as a supply vehicle. Bartholomew ordered the word Rosetta painted on the sides in large bold letters.

The temperature had been moderating, and the thermometer read 75 degrees Fahrenheit in Montana on the day of the supply pod launch. The rocket took off successfully from the Rosetta launch pad on an early August morning. The vehicle climbed to a height of one thousand feet when it exploded, leaving debris across Billings, Montana.

"Get me Homeland Security on the phone," Rosetta CEO Morgan said to Phil Duncan.

"Mr. Secretary, Frank Morgan here for Rosetta. To put it bluntly, sir, we're fucked. Our supply vehicle blew up a few moments after launch this morning. The two astronauts aboard *Stargazer* have only a few days of supplies left, after which they're out of luck. We're preparing another launch vehicle now, but it won't be ready for two weeks."

"Any indication of what happened to the rocket?" Bellamy asked.

'No, sir. We've launched dozens of those rockets over the years. It simply blew up at an altitude of 1,000 feet."

"This resupply mission was critical, as you well know, Frank. Does Rosetta have any suspicions about sabotage?"

"We have suspicions, Mr. Secretary, but we don't have any clues. We've already started an investigation. As you know, FBI agents are all over this place. But our critical mission now is to ready a resupply ship for another launch. Bill Cranston and Nancy Mullin are good people. It sickens me to think they may starve to death."

CHAPTER FORTY SIX

August 6

"Hey, smart lady, how many calories does a human being need to consume every day to stay alive?"

"I've been working on some numbers and they aren't making me happy," Nancy Mullin said. "To maintain current body weight, a woman needs to consume between 1,600 and 2,400 calories a day. A man needs between 2,000 and 3,000 to maintain his weight. No surprise that a man gets to hog the food. I worked these numbers with the supplies onboard, and we have about two weeks of food left. After that we can last for about a month. But even though we can last that long, we'll be in terrible shape. Our brains will be scrambled, and we'll suffer from delirium. If we survive much longer than that we'll have permanent brain damage. The resupply pod was supposed to arrive yesterday, and we know that didn't happen. So, things are going to get scary, and soon."

"*Stargazer* wasn't designed for reentry, but we may have to think about alternatives to starving in orbit," Bill Cranston said. "Because of the total communication blackout, we've got to make our own plans."

"Reentry isn't just risky, it's suicidal. *Stargazer* simply isn't designed for reentry. Here's what I think happened, Bill. Tell me if you agree. We have no idea how we lost communication, but it's a reality we've got to deal with, as well as the possibility that Rosetta can't fix the problem. If they could have, they would have. We can assume that something happened to the launch of the supply vehicle. They've launched dozens of those rockets, but logic tells us that something went wrong with the latest attempt. So, if I were Rosetta, I would launch another supply pod. There's no other choice. Either feed us or starve us. But it takes at least two weeks to outfit a supply pod and ready the launch vehicle. Since I've calculated that we'll run out of necessary food in about two weeks, I think it's fair to say we have a problem. Even if we go on a forced diet and consume fewer calories than required, we still could face starvation in a month. I hate to sound so negative, honey, but that's the way I see it."

"Besides being beautiful, Nance, you're brilliant. I agree with everything you've said. We need to keep our exercise to a minimum to help conserve calories."

"Does that mean we can't play Scrabble?"

"I'm afraid so, Nance. Just imagine our first game after we replenish our food."

"Stop thinking about it, handsome. You're consuming unnecessary calories. Let me hold your hand while we meditate. We have nothing else to do."

Although Cranston and Mullin didn't know it, the government had narrowed down the list of suspects. The question remained—was there enough time?

CHAPTER FORTY SEVEN

.

"It's the First Lady on line one for you, Mr. President."

"Hey, Dee, Are you on the way home?"

"I'm just boarding Marine One, Matt. I should be at the White House in a half hour. I miss you."

"And I miss you too, even though it's been only a week. Got something big to talk to me about?"

"Yeah, real big. Entirely *too* big."

***

At 4 p.m. the presidential helicopter, Marine One, landed on the South Lawn of the White House. Dee Blake walked across the lawn to the entrance to the White House escorted by three Marine guards and her two aides. She had just come from a secret meeting in Valhalla, New York. Although the title First Lady doesn't come with a list of specific duties, it's well known that Dee Blake is her husband's top aide and counsellor. When something top secret and sensitive needs to be done, it usually involves Dee.

Dee and Matt Blake met under unusual circumstances. Dee was a client of Chicago's top trial lawyer, Matt Blake. The case involved the wrongful death of her husband, investigative journalist Jim Spellman. What looked like an open-and-shut negligence case turned out to be a famous criminal matter, known around the world as the *Sideswipe Conspiracy*. The sideswipe collision that killed Dee's husband was proven to be murder, not a negligent act. Dee and Matt knew about Spellman's writings, and they became murder targets of the terrorist cell that was responsible for Jim Spellman's death. Because the threats against them turned out to be real, Dee and Matt became part of the FBI Witness Protection Program. While in a secret location in the program, Dee and Matt fell in love and married. As Dee would put it, you can't make up this shit.

The Blakes turned out to be America's favorite couple. It was no secret that both had gone through life-threatening bouts of alcoholism and drug addiction. It was no secret because Dee and Matt chose to be open about their struggles and spent a lot of their time helping others to slay their demons. In addition to her love for Matt, Dee also looked up to him as a leader. Dee would often tell people that. "I fell in love with a great guy and soon discovered that he was also a great man." Dee convinced Matt to run for President of the United States. He agreed, and toward the end of his campaign it looked like he would win easily. But his opponent, a sinister billionaire named Bartholomew Martin, organized a campaign of lies about Matt Blake. Martin won the election, based on fears he created about Matt Blake being soft on terrorism.

The Bartholomew Martin presidency turned out to be a threat to the foundations of American democracy. Every day a few liberties would disappear. Every day a new report would emerge of government spying on citizens. Accounts were frozen, assets seized, arrests were made, all without the familiar American institution of due process of law. "A knock on the door" became a fearful part of American reality. Martin's power grab was aided by his party's veto-proof majority in both houses of congress. After a few months, thoughtful people began to realize that America had elected its first dictator, Bartholomew Martin.

Never one to turn her back on a fight, Dee convinced Matt to try again for the White House. Along with a few close friends and confidants, Dee convinced Matt that he was the country's last hope for restoring democracy. She loved to quote her hero, Ronald Reagan: "Freedom is never more than one generation away from extinction."

Matt agreed to run again, and this time, with the country trembling in fear of its first dictator, he defeated Bartholomew Martin in a popular and electoral landslide.

***

"How about a kiss?" Matt said, as he wrapped his arms around Dee.

"Of course, big guy, but then I want to amaze you with what I've found out."

"Go ahead, amaze me?"

"You're not going to believe what I have to tell you."

They sat across from each other on the wing-back chairs with a coffee table in between. When talking to Dee, Matt never sat behind the executive desk.

"Two words, Matt—Bartholomew Martin. Rick Bellamy and I agreed that I would bring the news to you. It's so sensitive that Rick didn't want to talk over the phone."

Matt put his coffee cup on the table.

"From the look on your face, you don't seem surprised."

"I'm not. Go ahead, hon."

"You couldn't have picked a better Homeland Security Secretary. Rick Bellamy uncovers things that others would step over. His people, with appropriate subpoenas of course, tapped the phones and placed listening devices on Bartholomew Martin and his band of thugs who call themselves *The Reformers*, a name that you and I know well. They're currently located on a huge compound in Erbil, Kurdistan."

"Kurdistan, as you know, Dee, is really part of Iraq. The Kurds hate Bartholomew Martin and his people. They feed the CIA great information about the Reformers. You're right, Dee. Bellamy is the best. I didn't even have to tip him off to focus on Martin. He remembers the election where I beat Martin in a landslide. Bellamy remembered that Martin refused to concede and didn't even call to congratulate me after the results were clear. He also recalled the details about my kidnapping and the hijacking of our submarine. Remember the newspaper headline? 'The President is Missing.' I'll never forget the note I got from Bartholomew Martin when I returned to the White House. You remember it, Dee.

"The note said:

In keeping with the tradition I set for myself, I won't offer my congratulations, but only an observation. You somehow managed to pull it off again.
Until the next time,
Bartholomew Martin

"Well, it looks like 'the next time' has come. Martin loves to gloat, and his gloating is what put Bellamy on the case. Did Rick get into any specifics as to what Martin has to do with the crazy weather?"

"He got more than specific, Matt, he even has drilled down into the technical details. But then he hit a brick wall. I suggest that we meet with Rick Bellamy as soon as possible. The weather, as we all know, has moderated and is approaching normal. We have no idea what this means, but thanks to Bellamy, we know who to focus on."

"I understand that the *Stargazer* space station was supposed to be resupplied this week, but the supply rocket blew up right after it launched. That was the only rocket that Rosetta ever lost. What does Bellamy think about that, Dee?"

"Rick thinks that Martin and his people destroyed the rocket. Matt, The Reformers have taken the gloves off. Bartholomew Martin wants to occupy this office again, and it looks like he's ready to destroy a good part of the world to pull that off."

"Is anybody else in on these details?"

"I think you know me better than that, Matt. I'm the only one who knows about Bellamy's findings, and Rick wants to keep it that way."

"Do you think he's even kept it from his wife, Ellen? She's sharp as hell and a patriot to boot. I wonder if she knows about all of this."

"Although it hasn't been made public, Rick appointed Ellen as a deputy FBI agent, with Sarah Watson's full support. Discretion is in her DNA, Matt. If she knows something don't expect to see it on *The Ellen Bellamy Show*, unless it's an intentional hook to drag out some information from a guest. Although nobody knows it, especially the management at NBC, Ellen often uses lures that Rick gives her to get information for the government. They remind me of us—they're a team."

CHAPTER FORTY EIGHT

August 8

"How about a road trip, hon, specifically tomorrow?" I said to Ellen.

"I'm booked solid for the next two weeks, Rick. Some heavy-hitters are scheduled to be on the show. I don't see how I can get away. Where's the destination, anyway?"

"The White House. President Blake specifically requested that you be with me. I'm sure the president knows that I've brought you in on everything that's going on. Because you're a deputy FBI agent, you have top-secret clearance. Besides that, you also have the blessed 'need to know,' the other key to unlock the secret drawer. You need to know because *I need you to know*. Just like Dee Blake is to Matt Blake, you're my top advisor. I need you to know what's going on, so you can help me figure it out. Matt once told me that you remind him of Dee. I'd take that as quite a compliment. I know that nobody can take your place, but your producers have a mile-deep list of people wanting to sit in for you, although nobody's got a dimple as cute as yours."

"Obviously, I can't refuse, Rick. Is there anything new on the *Stargazer* issue that I should know about?"

"Yes. We just found out about this, and it's not pleasant. It seems that the *Stargazer* is in a total communication blackout. Neither the Rosetta Corporation nor the United States government can connect with the station. Another major issue is that the food supply rocket that was due to launch blew up a couple of minutes after take-off. The Rosetta people tell me that the two astronauts have at most a couple of weeks of food left. Unless they can be resupplied those two will die of starvation, a pretty nasty way to go. We're almost certain that this is an intentional act. Somebody wants the *Stargazer* to fail, just like somebody wants to screw with the world's weather."

"I suppose I shouldn't ask this, Rick, but do we have any idea who's behind this stuff?"

"I'll give you a hint. He was the 46th President of the United States."

"Bartholomew Martin?"

"The one and only."

"Holy shit."

"I agree, holy shit. First, he tried to turn the country into his own private kingdom, and now he wants to control the weather. Bartholomew Martin is the most dangerous man the country has ever faced, and he's showing no signs of retiring with his wealth. A lot of people think that he's painted a target on Matt Blake's back. When Blake defeated him in a landslide, Martin launched a never-ending vendetta. Martin wants President Blake out, and he's willing to destroy the world to pull it off. The only people who know that Martin is behind all this shit is you, me, the Blakes, and of course, Buster."

"Bartholomew Martin has two big problems on his hands, Rick—you and me. Let's nail that prick."

"Yes, let's nail him. I can picture him in Kurdistan now, composing the next act in his opera."

CHAPTER FORTY NINE

August 9

"Douglas, please give me your report on the replacement supply pod for *Stargazer*."

"We're right on schedule, Bartholomew. When the pod is within about 2,000 feet of *Stargazer* they will be able to communicate using shortwave radio. The launch is scheduled for the day after tomorrow."

"Weather permitting?" Martin said, laughing.

"Two of our own astronauts will be on the mission," Douglas said, "Mark Jackson and Jerome Laub. Because everybody involved speaks English with an American accent, I don't expect that they will arouse any suspicions."

"After they're done onloading the supplies, Douglas, what will be the mission for Jackson and Laub?"

"They will take over as the *Stargazer* astronauts."

"And what will become of Cranston and Mullin?"

"They will be killed, and their bodies disposed of in space. Jackson and

Laub will use pistols with silencers and blunt bullets. Despite conventional wisdom, handguns work perfectly well in a weightless environment. Because of the blunt bullets and the closeness of the firing positions, we're not worried about a round ricocheting and piercing the skin of the spacecraft."

"Have you prepared for the likelihood that Rosetta will realize that its astronauts have been replaced?"

"When we reopen the communications, it will be by text communication only. We'll explain that we want to use written messages to avoid mistakes. Rosetta will never know that its astronauts were terminated and, with our own men in place, we'll be ready to command the satellites."

"Excellent, Douglass. It will be the beginning of a new world. Alert me when the launch is about to take place. I want to be in our media room to observe it. Our mission will soon be accomplished."

CHAPTER FIFTY

August 10

"Bill, radar shows an object approaching us about five miles away, probably a spacecraft."

"*Stargazer, Stargazer*, this is *Food Truck One*, come in please," came the voice over the shortwave radio.

Bill Cranston was about to reply when Nancy Mullin grabbed his hand and shook her head.

"Since when did they give a supply pod a cute name? In the past they always had simple identifiers like Unit 250."

"Good point, Nance. I'll ask them about it."

"No, don't do that. I think we should play along. I'm having a strange feeling about this resupply pod. Just tell them you can hear them."

"*Food Truck One, this is Stargazer*, read you loud and clear, over."

"My name is Mark Jackson, am I speaking to Bill Cranston?"

"Yes, you are, Mark. Bill Cranston here."

Cranston turned to Nancy Mullin. "I don't remember any astronaut with that name at Rosetta."

"My fellow astronaut is Jerry Laub. We're both new, and that's why you probably haven't heard our names before."

Bill Cranston looked at Nancy Mullin. The both shrugged, not sure what that information could mean to them.

"We're 2,000 feet away," Jackson said. "You should be able to see us. I plan to approach the docking port of *Stargazer* slowly. Once we're docked we'll all form a chain gang to bring the supplies aboard."

"I have you on visual, Mark. It's a different kind of supply pod from what I've seen before."

"You know Rosetta, Bill. They like to change things all the time."

Nancy shook Cranston's sleeve.

"Look at the marking on the fuselage. Somebody forgot how to spell Rosetta."

Cranston looked at *Food Truck One*, this time more closely. On the side of the ship was the word, "Rosatta."

"Somebody's fucking with us, Nance. I'm guessing whoever it is shot down the first supply rocket from Montana and launched one of their own. The communication blackout enabled them to pull it off. Whoever the hell it is wants to take over this operation. That could explain the erratic behavior of the satellites and the weird weather events."

"What can we do about it, Captain Bill?" Nancy asked. "Think like the Marine you used to be."

Cranston reached into a locker next to the microphone and pulled out a Colt 45 pistol equipped with a sound suppression device. He inserted a magazine and chambered a round. The magazine holds seven rounds.

"What the hell are you going to do with that?"

"Possibly shoot a couple of people. Here's your gun. I've seen you on the firing range, and I know that you can use this thing. Now listen to me. As soon as you see a knife or a gun, shout the word 'weapon' at the top of your lungs. I'll do the same if I see it first. Shoot the man closest to you in mid-torso, and I'll do the same for the other one. Fire two rounds, no more, no less. After we take care of our friendly deliverymen we'll set their bodies loose into space. It's clear as crystal. They're here to kill us, Nance. We have no other option but to kill them first."

"Oh, dear God, Bill, I'm scared out of my mind. A fucking gunfight?"

"Nancy, look at me. Our lives are on the line, and we don't have a choice. To be blunt, we have to kill or be killed."

Mark Jackson maneuvered *Food Truck One* up to the docking station on *Stargazer,* gently locking it into place. He opened the airtight door and the two of them floated onto *Stargazer.* The entry room was nine by twelve feet. Bill Cranston stood three feet from one side of the door and Nancy stood three feet on the other side. They both held their pistols at their sides. As soon as they entered *Stargazer,* and sooner than Cranston and Mullin expected, both new astronauts drew guns. Nancy screamed, "*WEAPON,*" and fired two rounds into Mark Jackson, as Bill Cranston shot Laub twice. The sound suppression devices on the guns muffled the roar of the shots.

"Let's bring our deliverymen friends to the starboard hatch and give them a proper space burial."

Cranston put on his space suit and entered the airlock that led out into space. He grabbed the edge around the hatch to give himself leverage and pushed each of the bodies with all the strength in his legs, propelling them away from *Stargazer.* He knew that Nancy wouldn't like to see dead bodies floating around the station, and neither would he.

It took them an hour to transfer all the supplies and put them in the cabinets on *Stargazer.* They both agreed that *Food Truck One* would remain attached to *Stargazer.* The visiting supply vehicle, unlike *Stargazer,* was designed for reentry, something that they may have to think about.

"Hey, Nance, why the sourpuss?"

"I never killed anybody before. It's a creepy feeling."

"Look at it this way; if they killed you there wouldn't be any feeling at all. Good shooting, captain."

"Thanks, captain, you too. Let's celebrate our gunfight with a nice home cooked meal."

"I think I'll skip the saltines."

***

After they ate, they inspected the supply pod, *Food Truck One*.

"Check this out, Bill. It seems that they didn't communicate by voice but only by text messages. This message came in five minutes ago:

"Awaiting your report on the docking with *Stargazer*. Was there any resistance? Report immediately."

"Any *resistance?*" Nancy said. "I don't feel bad about shooting those scumbags anymore. The communications blackout was bullshit. They chose to use written messages only to preserve the appearance that we're not dead. Since they fucked with our heads, let's return the favor. Let's tell them the operation was a success and we're awaiting further orders."

"Hold on, Nance. Once the conversation gets two layers deep, they'll know they aren't speaking to their people. Then what? Will they launch another hit squad? Let's look through every piece of correspondence and see if we learn something. They won't freak out if we take a little while longer to reply to their most recent post. Let's read further."

"Oh, my God," Nancy said. "Look at this."

CHAPTER FIFTY ONE

"Are you sure it's a good idea to have a space station expert on my show?" Ellen asked.

"It's a fabulous idea, hon. It will be great for your ratings, and the country will thank you."

"Why would the country thank me?"

"Because the show will be pure bullshit. I know you don't like that idea, but the White House has specifically requested this, and the chief of staff filled me in on the guy. He's a professor at MIT and a former astronaut. He'll tell you everything he knows about space stations, which is a lot. He'll also toss a few curve balls. The idea is to throw Bartholomew Martin and company off. It's critical that Martin doesn't suspect that the government knows what he's up to."

"Do *we* know what he's up to?" Ellen asked.

"That's part of the idea. We'll not only throw him off, but we'll put him on the wrong scent. It will take a lot of intelligence gathering, but Buster, my favorite CIA spook, will be on the case."

***

"Good afternoon ladies and gentlemen and welcome to *The Ellen Bellamy Show*. The whole country has been up in the air recently about the American space station, *Stargazer*. We know that it monitors a group of 20 satellites, and it also tests and directs them to perform functions. *Stargazer* is owned and operated by the Rosetta Corporation, an American company. Recently, *Stargazer* has become a household word nationwide because of its part in the weather catastrophe. We know that after a series of satellite tests, the weather suddenly changed dramatically, giving us freezing temperatures and a record blizzard in the summer. Another test was performed, and the deepfreeze changed into a heat wave, with catastrophic flooding from the melting snow, not to mention tornados. Recently, the weather has moderated, and the temperatures across the country are normal. Here in New York City it's 82 degrees Fahrenheit, what you would expect for the month of August. But the big question that everybody wants answered is why this all happened. Our special guest today is Michael Crawford, a full professor at the MIT School of Engineering. Professor Crawford was one of the original crew of astronauts aboard the *Stargazer* when it was first launched. Besides serving aboard the *Stargazer*, he also headed up the research team that brought the first American space station into service. He was the commander of the first mission of the *International Space Station*. Welcome Professor Crawford."

"Thank you for having me on your show, Ellen. I used to avoid daytime television like the plague. That was before your show. Now I'm hooked at 3 p.m. every day."

"Thank for the vote of confidence, professor. Please tell us about *Stargazer.*"

"I'll tell you everything that I can, Ellen, but as you're aware, many of the details about *Stargazer* are top secret. *Stargazer*, the most recent operational space station, is similar in design to the *International Space Station*, or ISS, on which the Rosetta Corporation was the major contractor. *Stargazer*, is 240 feet long, 370 feet wide, and 70 feet high. It's capable of carrying a crew of six, but is currently manned by only two astronauts, Nancy

Mullin and Bill Cranston. They're both friends of mine, and both highly skilled engineers."

"Professor," Ellen said, "I don't think I'm stretching the truth when I say that the damned thing seems to be on the blink. Two tests went haywire, resulting in our lovely July and August blizzards when the satellites that *Stargazer* controls didn't respond properly to commands. And now we understand that communication broke down between *Stargazer* and the Rosetta Corporation, the station's owner. If signals from earth are being received by the station, we don't know it. It seems to be a communications blackout. How can that be professor?"

"Of one thing we're certain," Crawford lied, "the communications problems with *Stargazer* are completely natural, and not caused by anything on earth. It isn't unusual for a communications breakdown to occur between earth and a space station or satellite. As exciting as it may sound, nobody is causing this problem."

Ellen was amazed at the way Crawford lied so smoothly.

"Yesss," Rick Bellamy did a fist pump from his office where he was watching the show. "Did you catch that, Jake?" He said to the president's chief of staff who was on the phone. "This guy Crawford is perfect."

"The good news, professor, is that the temperatures have moderated across the country and are now close to normal," Ellen said. "But can anything be done about the communication blackout?"

"We'll need to exercise a lot of patience, Ellen. We can't change something that we don't control."

"What about food replenishment, professor? The astronauts can't go shopping at a nearby 7-11."

"I understand that a supply rocket will soon visit *Stargazer.*"

"But the resupply rocket blew up a few moments after takeoff," Ellen said.

"Of course, we all heard about that accident, but it only takes a few days to launch another supply vehicle," he lied.

Crawford answered questions for the next 15 minutes about life aboard a space station, holding back details when he thought he must.

"Thank you, Professor Crawford, for shining light on an increasingly dark subject."

***

"Crawford's a great guy," Rick said as Ellen walked into the apartment. "I want you to book him on your show for next week. He's the best source of disinformation we ever had."

"I have to admit that this stuff gives me the creeps, Rick. I get paid a ton of money to host my show, and here I am asking this guy questions that I know he's going answer with lies. "

"Hey, babe, you, me, Crawford, and a lot of other people share a common trait. We're American patriots, and if that means sometimes playing hardball with the facts, so be it. Bartholomew Martin and his turds wouldn't hesitate to slit our throats if the opportunity presented itself. So, what if we're using your show to mind fuck some horrible characters?"

"You're right, Rick. I just like to hear it from you to make my conscience clear. When it comes to Bartholomew Martin, I'd rather shoot the bastard than have people lie on my show, but we have to do what we have to do."

"Look at it this way, hon—you're just asking questions. Crawford's the one who's doing the lying."

"I'm worried about something, Rick. We may be doing a good job of confusing the Reformer thugs, but what about those two astronauts on *Stargazer*? They're real live people, and they're the ones who will take the hit if Martin figures out that we're on to him."

CHAPTER FIFTY TWO

August 12

"This whispering sucks, Bill."

"But we have to assume that whoever is responsible for this shit can hear our every word. I'm sure this *Food Truck* is laced with bugs we can't find. We can talk freely when we're aboard *Stargazer*, but not here on *Food Truck*. I'm going to take a wild guess that the communications blackout, if there ever was one, is caused by the same pricks who sent the assassins to resupply us. We've got to keep them in the dark as much as possible. Let me read those papers you gave me."

"You're going to freak out, hon."

"I can't believe what I'm reading, Nance," Bill said after reading just two pages. "Whoever's running this show is planning to take over the entire control of *Stargazer*. That's why those two guys wanted to kill us. They were the new management team."

"Unit 359, Unit 359, this is Homebase, come in," came the words over the console in *Food Truck One*.

"The home office is calling, and they're not using the words *Food Truck*.

So much for the communications blackout lies." Nancy whispered. "We've got to come up with some convincing bullshit—fast."

"Here, I'll put the shortwave radio on high squelch to answer them. They won't notice a different voice over the static."

"This is Unit 359," Cranston said, his radio providing static cover. "I'm having a difficult time hearing you, Homebase. There's a lot of static as you can probably hear."

"I understand, 359. I'll speak slowly."

"Hey Nance, that doesn't sound like Duncan. I thought only he could communicate with us."

"Who am I speaking to?" Douglas Merriman asked.

Nancy handed Bill a piece of paper with two names on it.

"This is Mark Jackson," Cranston said.

"And I'm Douglas Merriman. I've been told to communicate directly with you. We need your report on the mission as of right now. Has the situation with the two astronauts been, uh, handled?"

Bill and Nancy looked at each other. "Why aren't we speaking to Duncan?" Nancy whispered.

"The astronaut situation has been taken care of," Bill Cranston said. "Jerry Laub and I are in command."

"Say again, Mark, you're breaking up."

The radio static was doing its job.

"I said that the existing astronaut situation has been handled, Douglas. They're both dead. Jerry Laub and I are in sole command."

"That's great news, Mark. I assume that the controls on *Stargazer* are the same as what you've been studying for a month. Are you guys prepared to begin the satellite test sequence?"

"Please repeat, you're breaking up," Bill said, trying to buy some time.

"Now what the hell do we do, Nance?" Bill whispered. "Remember what happened last time we tested the satellites?"

"We've got to follow their orders, or we'll blow the whole thing."

"I asked if you're prepared to execute a satellite test pattern. Do you read me?"

"Yes, I read you, Douglas, if not loud and clear."

"Okay, Mark, one by one, I want you to test each of the 20 satellites, including the solar panels."

Bill and Nancy began the satellite tests.

"Hey, Nance, why isn't Duncan the one speaking to us?" Bill whispered.

"Beats me, but we know we're communicating with Rosetta. Just another little mystery."

CHAPTER FIFTY THREE

August 14 – The Blizzard Returns

"Good afternoon, ladies and gentlemen, I'm your host, Ellen Bellamy, sporting my new suntan. Today we're going to discuss a pleasant topic, one that hasn't been much fun to talk about recently. Al Roker, the world's favorite weatherman, is here with me to discuss the beautiful August weather we're enjoying. Al, please tell us the good news."

"Recently you've heard me talk about the new meteorology, Ellen, a science that has recently been unable to live up to its mission—to forecast the weather. For almost a month no meteorologist on earth could tell you what to expect, other than by using radar, which is nowhere near as accurate as satellites for long range predictions. This time period will forever be known for the strangest weather on record. We saw temperatures in the low single digits and even a monstrous blizzard. For the past few days, however, we seem to have caught a break. Temperatures worldwide are at or near normal for this time of year, with a few exceptions of course, which is to be expected. Here in New York City at 3:05 p.m. on a beautiful August 14, the thermometer reads a delightful 82 degrees Fahrenheit, and the black ice has been replaced by water puddles."

***

"Two down and eighteen to go, Nance. The next satellite we're about to test is the one where the shit hit the fan last time. Here we go into the wild blue yonder."

***

"Al, are you willing to go on the hook with a forecast for the rest of the week?"

"My parents raised a positive thinker, so yes, Ellen, I'm willing to give you a forecast. For the Northeast United States, it's more warm temperatures and beautiful sunshine. Over the past month I've joked that the only reliable weather tools at my disposal were my window and my telephone. Well, our long-range radar, one of our trusted forecasting tools, tells us that the same delightful weather that we're experiencing now will continue. It's not as accurate for the long-range forecasting as a satellite prediction, but the news looks good."

Both Al Roker and Ellen Bellamy grabbed their earpieces as their producer screamed into their ears.

"Look out the fucking window, Al, and tell the audience what you see," yelled the producer. "Snow, and a lot of it. The thermometer on our roof reads 31 degrees."

"You folks often hear me say to look outside your window, and that's exactly what I'm about to do, as my producer just suggested while yelling into my earpiece."

When the camera turned to the window, Roker flipped his producer a middle finger.

Roker walked up to the window, which rattled from a fierce wind. Swirling sheets of snow blew against the glass.

"I often wish that I could do a show that I could rehearse for, one where I show up and just go through the scenes that I had rehearsed. Weather reporting isn't like that, as you can see by looking through our studio

150

window. A couple of minutes ago I was happily gushing about our beautiful weather. Now I'm told that our rooftop thermometer reads 31 degrees Fahrenheit, 68 degrees colder than when I started this segment 15 minutes ago. I just looked at my radar screen, and contrary to what it showed a few minutes ago, we are covered by thick clouds, obviously bearing snow. So, the radar is working, but we just can't use it for reporting good news. And here's the scary part: our Doppler radar didn't see this front coming because it happened so fast. There's been no change in our satellite situation, which remains the same—no contact with the satellites. Our research reporters tell us that the situation is similar all over the globe, rapidly dropping temperatures, and in many places, heavy snow. So, head to the closet and get out your winter clothes once again."

***

"Unit 359, this is Home Base, do you read?"

"Roger, Home Base, Unit 359 here, but we still have heavy static," Bill Cranston said, hoping the guy on the other end didn't realize that he wasn't speaking to Mark Jackson.

"Mark, I want you to hit the override switch on the main console."

"Holy shit," Nancy whispered, "the switch is malfunctioning again. Tell them we just tried it and it doesn't work."

"We've just discovered that the override switch doesn't respond, Douglas. The satellites are going through their configurations and there's no way to stop them. Is it affecting the weather on earth?"

"Let us worry about the situation on earth."

CHAPTER FIFTY FOUR

August 15

"Mr. President, when you ran for office did you expect that you would be giving so many weather reports?"

"Very funny, Jake," the president said to his chief of staff. "Update me on our rescue mission for *Stargazer*."

"As you ordered, sir, we're keeping this plan as secret as possible. I'm dealing directly with Roger Palmer, the administrator of NASA. He knows that all communications between NASA and the rest of the government will come directly through me to you. Only nine people in total are involved in this operation. We believe that a ship from another entity, probably Bartholomew Martin's people, has docked with the *Stargazer*. As you know, there is still a total communications blackout with *Stargazer*. We don't know the fate of the two Rosetta astronauts. Our objective is to get close enough to *Stargazer* so we can communicate directly by shortwave radio."

"What do you expect to find, if not the two astronauts?"

"Depending on what we find, sir, it could be a violent confrontation. But our ship, called *Ranger*, will pack enough firepower to come out on top. *Ranger* will have six people aboard, all heavily armed SEALs, well experienced in close combat. If we find William Cranston and Nancy Mullin aboard and safe, we will relieve them with two new astronauts after they get checked out on the *Stargazer* controls."

"Correct me if I'm wrong," the president said. "The craft that docked with *Stargazer* is considered hostile. If so, how can Cranston and Mullin be safe?"

"Cranston and Mullin are both smart and they're also a couple of tough cookies, to put it bluntly, Mr. President. Cranston was a Marine captain and engaged in combat in both Iraq and Afghanistan. Mullin was a captain in the Air Force and saw combat in a firefight in Afghanistan. These people aren't a couple of yokels that can be rolled over easily. They're both armed with Colt 45s. We think it's unlikely that a hostile force could take over *Stargazer* without getting into a serious mix-up with Cranston and Mullin, but obviously we don't know the result for certain."

"I want our Homeland Security head, Rick Bellamy, on the inside of this mission. His wife, Ellen, is more than a TV star, she's a sharp lady with a top-secret clearance. Think of her as Rick's partner, which she is in more ways than one."

He looked over Jake Arnold's shoulder and pointed.

"What the hell is that?" He said.

"Oh, dear God, Mr. President, it looks like snow. I guess you'll be giving another weather report soon."

"Okay, wise guy, get me up to speed on what this is all about. Call Bellamy's office first. He has a way of being on top of things before anyone else."

"Yes, sir. Should I alert the First Lady?"

"No, I'll call her. She's taking a well-deserved nap after her trip."

***

"Hi Dee, I hope I didn't wake you."

"Don't worry about it, hon, I need to get up anyway. Holy shit. Have you looked out the window?"

"Yes. I wanted to ask you if you cared for a sleigh ride."

"I'll take a quick shower and I'll be right down. Something tells me we have another crisis to talk about."

"More than that, hon. Jake and I will bring you up to speed when you get there."

"Let me guess—it has to do with *Stargazer*."

"To think that I married you for your looks."

CHAPTER FIFTY FIVE

August 16

"Good morning, gentlemen, I'm Navy SEAL Commander Mike Patterson. I will be in command of our mission aboard the *Ranger*. Our objective is to board *Stargazer* and possibly rescue its crew, astronauts William Cranston and Nancy Mullin. Our job is to bring the astronauts back to earth. Lieutenants Frank Wilson and Jack Simmons will take over as the new crew for *Stargazer*. The other three of you will serve as a possible combat team, although we hope it won't come to that. As you've already been briefed, the *Stargazer* is in a communications blackout, or at least we think she is. Our intelligence tells us that another supply pod docked with *Stargazer*. We believe that the replacement pod is hostile and is manned by two people. We will encounter one of two scenarios. First, astronauts Cranston and Mullin engaged the hostiles and killed them. They're both combat tested military veterans. The other scenario is that the two hostiles killed Cranston and Mullin. If the hostiles are in control, our job is to kill them and take over the station. When we get close to

Stargazer we will communicate by shortwave radio. We've all listened to hours of recordings of the voices of Cranston and Mullin, so it should be easy to tell who's running *Stargazer*. If we determine that the hostiles are in control, we'll have a problem. So, this operation will either be a pleasant reunion with a couple of fine Americans, or a combat mission to kill the enemy. We board *Ranger* at 0800 tomorrow morning and launch at 0845. Any questions?"

"Commander," asked Frank Wilson, "since the snowy weather has returned, are there any concerns about launching into a blizzard?"

"Ever since the *Challenger* exploded after takeoff a few years ago, our entire space establishment has been focused on weather and flight protocols. As of now, we're good to go in the shittiest weather you can imagine. I'm much more concerned about a possible gunfight than I am the weather. We'll meet here in the briefing room at 0730 and then head to the launch pad. Lock and load, gentlemen."

CHAPTER FIFTY SIX

August 17

"Mr. Secretary, Jake Arnold here at the White House. The president asked me to let you know that your trip to Washington is off. It's too dangerous to fly during this wicked blizzard. The meeting will be conducted from the White House Situation Room, so it will be totally secure. Please arrange for your wife Ellen to be with you and call us at noon today. The circumstances have heated up to say the least."

***

"We're going on offense, Rick," President Blake said. "We're about to launch an extremely dangerous mission with our heads partially up our asses. As you know, Commander Mike Patterson will head a team of six SEALs to connect with *Stargazer*. Their craft is known as *Ranger*. Because of the communication blackout, we're not sure of the status of Cranston and Mullin, Rosetta's two astronauts on *Stargazer*. We know that a hostile craft has docked with the station. What we don't know is the outcome. The two possibilities are that the hostiles boarded *Stargazer* and killed Cranston and Mullin. The second possibility, a strong one, is that Cranston and Mullin engaged the hostiles and killed *them*. We won't know until Commander Patterson and his people attempt to board."

"Mr. President," I said, "our people feel confident that Cranston and Mullin pulled it off. They're both tough as nails, and they know when something is out of line. It will be a tense situation when Commander Patterson and his men attempt to board. They will first try to communicate with *Stargazer* when they're close to the ship, using shortwave radio. Patterson's first job is to convince them that he and his team are on the right side. The last thing we want is a fire fight between two friendly groups."

"Rick, Dee Blake here. I've researched the situation to death and I've concluded that firing weapons will present a minimum danger. Contrary to common belief, gunfire is possible in a weightless environment. The bullets are fired with spring action and the lack of gravity is not an issue. But we still don't know who came out on top in a gunfight between the hostiles and our astronauts."

***

"Now what?" Bill Cranston said. "Any guesses?"

"My hunch is that whoever is running this show is aware that their mission failed. I think they'll try to launch another resupply craft. But it's also likely, 100 percent likely, that our government will launch a craft as well. President Blake is not about to sit on his ass and hope for the best. He has a well-earned reputation as a tough SOB. I'm guessing that an American ship will be headed our way shortly."

"I agree, but what if the enemy launches another supply ship at the same time? When we see another supply pod approach, you and I will have to make a quick decision whether to open fire or spread a welcome mat."

"Hey, Bill, don't you Marines have a bunch of passwords that you use for a situation like this, a password to identify a good guy?"

"Yes, but it changes all the time. All I need to hear is one of the code words we used in Afghanistan and we'll know if our visitors are friendly. We have to assume that the hostiles are not so deep inside that they know the words too."

"While we're waiting, let's work on our wedding guest list," Nancy said.

"You make it easy to love you, Nance. We're not sure we'll make it out of this alive, and you want to work on a guest list. I've already started mine. Let's compare notes."

"Hey, handsome, check out your 45. It looks like the safety's off."

"Yes, ma'am. Shall I salute you or give you a kiss?"

CHAPTER FIFTY SEVEN

August 18

The snow blew constantly at the Kennedy Space Center in Titusville, Florida. The temperature was relatively moderate, relative to the strange times, with a thermometer reading of 31 degrees Fahrenheit.

Major Jack Whalen was the pilot for the upcoming mission. Commander Mike Patterson was the overall commander of the operation. The plan was to launch at 0845 and rendezvous with *Stargazer* four hours after takeoff.

President Blake and First Lady Dee watched the event from the Situation Room at the White House, along with Chief of Staff Jake Arnold. Ellen and I were patched into the White House from my office. Sarah Watson joined us. The camera was stationed a quarter mile from the launch pad, but the blowing snow made visibility terrible. I popped another Maalox into my mouth.

"I keep reminding myself that bad-weather space launches are becoming a common practice," the President said, "but looking at that rocket through the snow scares the hell out of me."

The voice from Mission Control at the Kennedy Space Center was both familiar, and, given the weather conditions, ominous.

"T minus five, four, three, two, one, we have ignition."

The three main rocket engines together provide almost 1.2 million pounds of thrust and the two solid rocket boosters provide a total of 6.6 million pounds more. The total thrust at takeoff is about 7.8 million pounds, enough to launch a rocket and enough to blow snow in every direction.

Not a word was spoken at the White House or Federal Plaza in New York. Finally, President Blake broke the silence.

"In a little under four hours we'll know where we stand," the president said. "*Ranger* will approach *Stargazer*, and we expect to see the hostile spacecraft docked to it. Once we open shortwave radio communication, we'll know if we're going into combat or a welcoming party."

Stargazer appeared in view from *Ranger* as the ship approached.

"We can see the answer to our first question," the President said. "Another spacecraft is docked with *Stargazer*. Hey, how the hell do you spell Rosetta?"

"Good news so far, Mr. President," Rick Bellamy said. "That dumb spelling error should have alerted Cranston and Mullin that something wrong was about to happen."

***

"Nance, take a look," Bill Cranston said. "We're being approached by another spacecraft. Look at the words painted on the fuselage—United States of America."

"And they didn't even misspell it," Nancy said. "I expect to hear a message on the radio shortly."

"*Stargazer, Stargazer*, this is United States Spacecraft *Ranger*, Navy SEAL Commander Mike Patterson speaking. Come in please and identify yourself."

"I'm astronaut Nancy Mullin and I'm here with Bill Cranston."

The entire conversation was transmitted from *Ranger* to the loudspeakers at the White House and my office in New York. When Nancy Mullin identified herself, all of us totally freaked out—cheers, tears, and fist pumps.

"And I'm astronaut and Marine Corps reservist Bill Cranston. Commander, did you serve in Afghanistan?"

"Yes, I did."

"So, if I said 'who goes there' I would expect to hear one of the secret code words. Do you have one for me, sir?"

"*Bugaloo*, Mr. Cranston. I hope that word is good enough."

Bill gave Nancy a thumbs-up sign.

"Before I explain our plans, please tell me what happened to the two astronauts who docked the misspelled Rosetta pod."

"They came aboard with guns drawn," Nancy said, "but they weren't fast enough. We shot them both and launched their bodies into space."

The president's situation room and my office once again broke out into happy bedlam.

"Please tell us your plans, commander," Nancy said.

"My orders are to relieve you both after your successful mission and to take you back with us on *Ranger*. I have five men with me. Two will remain aboard *Stargazer* and take command. You folks will join us for our return to Kennedy Space Center. Please let me know how you wish me to proceed. I understand that you have reasonable security concerns after the last time you were visited."

"Commander, please enter *Stargazer* through the supply pod that's attached. We'll unlock it for you. I know that you are armed, obviously, so please enter the main compartment with your weapons held in front of you pointed backward. Bill Cranston and I will have our guns trained on you. I assure you that we're well experienced in the use of firearms. After we've collected your weapons and are satisfied that you're friendlies, we'll then invite you to join us for lunch after returning your guns to you. Then I'm going to ask each of you to sign your name on a pad, making sure it's legible, and include your mailing addresses and phone numbers. You will be the first people on our guest list."

"Guest list?" Patterson asked.

"Yes, Bill and I are inviting you all to our wedding to be held in the very near future."

After the six men came aboard *Stargazer*, Nancy said "You guys look a little green."

"Well, except for our two relief astronauts here, the rest of us have never been in space before," Commander Patterson said. "I think I'll just have cheese and crackers for lunch."

They heard a voice over the loudspeaker. "Please stand by for the President of the United States," Jake Arnold said.

"The fact that you can hear me tells us that the communication black-out has ended, if it ever existed in the first place," President Blake said "We're all breathing easier after what we've just heard. I congratulate all of you on a successful mission, and I congratulate you, Bill and Nancy, on your upcoming wedding. You give a new meaning to the word crewmates. Command of *Stargazer* is now under the United States government. The Rosetta Corporation, no matter how you spell it, is still out of communication with *Stargazer*, or at least we think it is. I'm going to turn the microphone over to Phil Duncan, Operations VP of Rosetta, who is standing next to me. Using White House equipment, he's going to work with you on sending signals to your satellites. Our simple objective is to stop this August blizzard and return our weather to something approximating normal. Enjoy your lunch. We'll speak again shortly."

Duncan worked with the astronauts, existing and new, on getting the satellites under control.

***

"The President is back on the line, Rick," Jake Arnold said.

"Rick, I'm sure we'd love to say, 'and they all happily lived thereafter,' but we know that's anything but the truth. Bartholomew Martin is the essence of evil, and nothing brings out his evil more than when he's thwarted in one of his missions. It's obvious that he wants to take control of *Stargazer*, and then take control of the world's weather. Nobody, including the people at Rosetta, knows exactly how he wants to do it, but what he's done with the weather so far shows that he's on his intended path. Nothing will stop this guy but blunt force, which is exactly what I aim to give him. We've got to stop this bastard before he succeeds in his original goal. Ever since I beat him in the election, he's wanted revenge, and to use our country to deliver it. He tried to create America's first dictatorship and came damn close. I'm not going to give that fuck another chance another chance."

Dee gave the president a disapproving look when he used the word "fuck."

CHAPTER FIFTY EIGHT

August 19

Bill Cranston and Nancy Mullin boarded *Ranger* for their trip back to earth. They strapped themselves into their seats, along with the other four members of the flight. Major Jack Whalen, pilot and commander of the reentry flight, handed them a message.

"Looks like Rosetta can't wait to see us, Bill. This note says that a private jet will meet us at Orlando International Airport, not far from Kennedy Space Center. The plane will take us to New York, where we'll be debriefed by Homeland Security Secretary Rick Bellamy. Wow. After our debriefing, they're putting us up at the presidential suite at the Waldorf Astoria. We're scheduled to take off for Rosetta headquarters the next day. Looks like you and I are hot shit."

"Get ready for a fun ride, folks," pilot Jack Whalen said, "especially our guests of honor, Bill and Nancy. We're going to slow from a speed of 25,000 mph to a subsonic speed so that we don't turn into a burnt marshmallow. We'll begin reentry into the earth's atmosphere at about 62 miles above the surface of the earth. My job is to hit the right angle. Too high and we burn up. Too low and we bounce off the earth's atmosphere like a rock skimming off the surface of a lake. As we descend, our speed will be further reduced when I deploy our drogue parachutes. All told it will be about three hours and twenty minutes from the time we undocked from *Stargazer* to the time we touchdown in a big field near the space center. I'm sorry, but meal service is not available in economy class. Enjoy the ride."

CHAPTER FIFTY NINE

August 20

"Have you ever flown in weather like this, Bill?"

"Yes, but never in a Lockheed C-141 Starlifter. This monster makes the wind a gentle breeze. I'm amazed they ordered this plane just for the two of us to fly to Billings."

"Hey, don't be so humble, Bill. With all the crazy shit that's been going on, you and I are hot stuff. Senior management is going to want to talk to us forever."

"To change the subject," Bill said, "how did you enjoy our stay at the Waldorf last night?"

"Never in a million years would I have thought that making love in a gravity environment beats the hell out of doing it weightless," Nancy said as she squeezed his hand. "Maybe it has something to do with traction. I hate to say, 'back to work,' but that's where we're headed. Phil Duncan told me to be prepared for endless debriefings."

"You just brought up a question in my mind, Nance. What do you think of Phil Duncan?"

"Phil seems like a good executive and he's easy to get along with. I think the big boss hangs on his every word."

"Did the thought ever cross your mind that Duncan controls a bit too much of Rosetta? I'm going to pose a question. Do you completely trust this guy?"

"You bring up a subject that has rattled around my brain from time to time," Nancy said. "Phil Duncan has been on the inside of every single satellite screwup. Sounds crazy, but it almost seems like he knew what was about to happen. And I still can't understand why we spoke to that guy Merriman rather than Duncan. But in answer to your question, yes, I trust the guy."

"I asked you if you trust Duncan *completely.* So, do you?"

"The answer is no, but I'm not sure where we're going with this."

"Let's just keep your answer in mind during our upcoming meetings. You answered 'no' when I asked if you trusted him completely. I think our circumstances require complete trust. Let's keep our ears and eyes open."

CHAPTER SIXTY

August 21

"We've lost communication with *Unit 359* and with *Stargazer*, Bartholomew," Douglas Merriman said. "Our engineers tell me that the plug was pulled by someone in our vehicle and isn't a result of anything normal."

"Tell me, Douglas, do you think the people we spoke to recently were our astronauts?"

"No, I'm now sure they weren't, Bartholomew. The static we heard on our conversations was intentional, I'm sure, and had nothing to do with normal conditions. I think the static was meant to mask the identity of the people we spoke to. I believe that they killed Laub and Jackson. The man I spoke to identified himself as Mark Jackson, but I'm sure that he was William Cranston, one of the Rosetta astronauts. To be blunt, our mission failed."

"Douglas, are you prepared to speak about our alternate plan?"

"Yes, sir."

"Sir?"

"I'm sorry, Bartholomew. In answer to your question, yes, I am ready to talk about our alternatives. A few months ago, we realized that all our plans were based on one thing, *Stargazer*. We knew that, although our technology was superior, the space station was under the command of two people who did not answer to us, the astronauts Cranston and Mullin. The two of them, especially Nancy Mullin, are more intelligent than we had given them credit for. Although our software was able to control the satellites from both Rosetta headquarters and *Stargazer*, we still had those two people in the way."

"Douglas, if you want to write a book, please do so, but in the meantime, do not answer my question with an encyclopedic response. So, tell me, in a few words, what is our best alternative?"

"The alternative is *Moonwalker,* our own space station, served by *Satstorm*, our utility rocket for supplies and repairs. *Moonwalker* is about 95 percent ready. Of course, it needs to be launched in parts and assembled in space, which will take approximately three trips by *Satstorm*."

"Douglas, you used the word 'approximately,' a heinous term. I do not work with approximate numbers, only exact ones."

"It will take no more than three trips by *Satstorm*, Bartholomew. The entire operation, from completion of *Moonwalker* to its assembly in space will take exactly two weeks."

"Tell me about our means of secrecy, Douglas. We cannot simply act on our plans for two weeks under the watchful eyes of the United States government."

"Our secrecy is the same source as our operations with *Stargazer,* Bartholomew. We have deeply imbedded four key people in the management of the Rosetta Corporation. Rosetta could never figure out how its satellites malfunctioned, but they weren't malfunctions at all, just commands that our insiders programmed into the software that controls the satellites. Our new space station, *Moonwalker*, as well as its service ship, *Satstorm*, are both manufactured by Rosetta."

"Who is our key insider at Rosetta, Douglas?"

"Philip Duncan, the vice president of operations. He is not only a decision maker, he is the right-hand executive to Frank Morgan, the CEO. Morgan never takes a step without discussing it with Duncan. It was Duncan who convinced Morgan to construct the additional space station and supply ship. Duncan also told us about our astronauts, Mark Jackson and Jerome Laub. Because their voices were obscured by static, Duncan was unable to determine who he was speaking to, nor was I in my conversation with them. Duncan later found out from the Rosetta astronauts themselves that they had killed Jackson and Laub in a gun fight. Cranston and Mullin, the Rosetta astronauts, have been returned to earth by a rescue spacecraft named *Ranger*. Our ship is still attached to *Stargazer*, and is manned by two newly assigned astronauts from the American government. Phil Duncan advises me that he will soon order the two new astronauts to perform satellite tests, although he may encounter interference from the government. Cranston and Mullin are accustomed to speaking to him, and it's essential that we do not compromise his identity."

"So, the most important item on our agenda will occur in two weeks." Bartholomew said. "We will destroy *Stargazer* and soon after that we will operate *Moonwalker*, our new space station, or to be more appropriate, Rosetta Corporation's new space station."

CHAPTER SIXTY ONE

August 22

"I'm out of here, Janey. I'll be gone for the rest of the day," General Roger Dolan, the Chairman of the Joint Chiefs of Staff, said to his assistant.

"May I ask where you'll be, sir?"

"I'm meeting the Thing with Two Heads."

"The what with which?"

"Potus and Flotus, Janey. The president and first lady work so closely they complete each other's sentences. I've been in the Army through five administrations, and I've never been as impressed as I am with those two. Dee Blake is a one-woman cabinet."

"Enjoy your meeting, sir, and please give the president and first lady my best. Better yet, how about getting an autographed picture for me?"

"See you tomorrow, wise guy."

***

"General Dolan is here for your meeting, Mr. President."

"Have a seat, General," I said. "How about a cup of coffee?"

"That would be great, Mr. President. I could use a jolt of caffeine."

"What we'll talk about today will be jolting enough. I believe you've met Dee before."

"Yes, sir. Good to see you, Madam First Lady."

"Just call me Dee, general. We have too much to talk about to get tripped up over titles."

"Our small gathering here today will be the most important meeting any of us has ever attended," President Blake said.

The general, spilling coffee down his chin, couldn't mask his surprise.

"I see that I've got your attention, general. You may want your next cup of coffee to be decaf. So, here's what's up. We're going to declare war shortly on a small country, actually not a country at all. Our goal will not be to negotiate a peace settlement. Our goal will be to eradicate the organization, to wipe it off the face of the earth, especially its leader. Any guess as to whom I'm talking about, general?"

"It can't be ISIS or al Qaeda, because we're already at war with those entities. My guess is that we're going to attack your predecessor, Bartholomew Martin, the slimiest scumbag on earth, along with his merry band of criminals called the Reformers. Please pardon my language, Dee."

"You guessed right, general. Tell me what you know about the group."

"We're intensely focused on Martin and his group, sir, because they are an obvious source of potential danger, and because you ordered us to concentrate on them. The size of the group is substantial, having grown to over 20,000 soldiers, if they can be described that way. They occupy a large area in Erbil, Kurdistan, about 10 square miles. Martin's pile of money guarantees him the loyalty of his people. Our research tells us that the average soldier makes over $50,000 per year, about what an Army captain earns in the U.S. They're well trained by former American soldiers. Their equipment includes 200 tanks. They have a small air group, not much to speak of, about 100 planes in total. They have virtually no navy, just a few gunboats."

"Have you prepared any preliminary battle plans, as you do with most potential adversaries?"

"Yes, sir. We've been laying out contingency battle plans against them for months. We'll begin with a crippling first strike including massive bombing raids and non-nuclear cruise missile attacks. Then we'll follow up the air strikes with armor and infantry attacks, which should be accurate because our imbedded spies gave us detailed maps of their entire compound. The Kurds, who seem to hate Martin's group more than they do the Iraqis, have been invaluable. We know where the ammunition is kept and where the troop barracks are located, as well as the heavy armor compound, and Martin's headquarters. Mr. President, don't worry about waging another political campaign against that bastard."

CHAPTER SIXTY TWO

August 22

"Shepard Smith for *Fox News* ladies and gentlemen. I have some shocking news to take our minds off our continuing August snowfall. In the early morning hours at 3 a.m. Eastern Time, the American space station, *Stargazer*, exploded into millions of pieces. There has been persistent speculation that *Stargazer* had something to do with the strange weather we've been experiencing for the past month. Our first encounter with mid-summer freezing temperatures came shortly after *Stargazer* performed a test of a satellite solar panel array. *Stargazer*, which was owned by the American Rosetta Corporation, became operational just a couple of years ago. Its main job was to enhance our GPS capabilities with a group of 20 satellites that also belonged to the company. The satellites were also tasked to provide weather forecasting, and I'll leave it to you to decide if they did a good job. A supply vehicle, the identity of which for some reason hasn't been disclosed, was connected to *Stargazer* when it exploded. I regret to say that two American astronauts lost their lives, Lieutenants Frank

Wilson of New York City and Jack Simmons of Stamford, Connecticut.

***

"Homeland Security Secretary on line one for you, Mr. President."

"Rick, do we know who blew up *Stargazer?*"

"I'm overstating the obvious when I say that an explosion in space doesn't leave fingerprints. We had no idea it was coming, and we're confused because if it's an enemy, such as Bartholomew Martin, who wants to attack us using weather satellites, blowing up the controlling space station doesn't make sense."

"But Rosetta's planning to set up a new space station, yes? Have you spoken to the Rosetta people?"

"Rosetta is in final stages of planning its new space station, *Moonwalker*, which they had scheduled to replace *Stargazer* eventually. The destruction of *Stargazer* has pushed the schedule forward. They tell me that the new platform will be ready in less than two weeks, including a process of launching it into space in parts and then assembling it."

"Rick, we all noticed that it has stopped snowing and the temperature is moderating. I understand that this pattern started in the early morning hours. Do you see any connection between the snow stopping and *Stargazer* blowing up?"

"Logic tells us that there is a connection, Mr. President, but we have no direct evidence, other than the timing of both events."

"My gut tells me that more coincidences are on their way, Rick. There are always coincidences when Bartholomew Martin is involved. These events were not flukes but deliberate actions."

CHAPTER SIXTY THREE

August 23

Nancy Mullin sat in the executive cafeteria at Rosetta Corporation waiting to have breakfast with her colleague and fiancé, Bill Cranston. Her eyes were focused on the TV on the wall. The anchorman was reporting the overnight explosion and destruction of *Stargazer*. Bill Cranston walked up to the table and sat.

"You heard the news, I'm sure," Nancy said.

"Yes, but I have other news, something that will freak you out. As I was walking down the corridor on my way here, I came upon Phil Duncan."

"He told you about the *Stargazer* explosion?"

"No. I heard about it on the radio. But all he said was 'good morning, Bill,' and smiled. That's all he said—*Good morning*. Something here isn't fitting together, Nance. If you're in charge of operating a space station that suddenly blows up, wouldn't you want to have a chat with one of the people who operated the damn thing until a few days ago? Wouldn't you have something to say beyond 'good morning'?"

Nancy put down her coffee mug and stared at Cranston.

"He made no mention of the *Stargazer* explosion?"

"Not a word."

Nancy rubbed her face with both hands trying to pull her thoughts together.

"Let's review some stuff, Bill. Each time we did the satellite tests that resulted in the weather madness, we were on linkup with Duncan. Each time he blamed it on something none of us knew anything about. In our phone conversations with him since we got back to earth, he never once discussed the communication problems with *Stargazer*, and he had no comment when we told him all about the unknown supply craft. He didn't even say anything when we told him about shooting two people. He showed the same amount of emotion as if we told him we ran over a fucking squirrel."

"Let's take this a bit further and do some speculating," Bill said. "Assume, for the sake of argument, that Phil Duncan is the missing insider. We screw up his plans for killing us, and then he sends another vehicle to blow up the space station that we recently abandoned. If you were Phil Duncan, what would you do next?"

"The answer is easy, Bill. I'd arrange for the deaths of Bill Cranston and Nancy Mullin. I think we need to make a phone call to Rick Bellamy from Homeland Security. He gave us his secure number. Let's go outside and make the call—while we're still alive."

***

"Mr. Secretary, it's Nancy Mullin calling for you on the secure line. She's the astronaut lady, yes?"

"I was just about to call you, Nancy," Bellamy said. "You've heard about the *Stargazer* explosion I assume."

"Yes, we have, Mr. Secretary. But beyond that, Bill Cranston and I have some concerns, some big concerns."

Nancy explained their suspicions about Phil Duncan, and said she feared they might be next on Duncan's hit list.

"Explain to me exactly where you are and stay there," Bellamy said. "Don't move. We have a few FBI agents at Rosetta. I'm going to contact the lead agent and have him meet you in a couple of minutes and get you the hell out of there. Before you board the plane you can text message Duncan with a story that you had to visit your ailing grandmother. You'll be coming to New York. I repeat, *do not move.*"

CHAPTER SIXTY FOUR

August 24

Air Force Lieutenant Colonel James Burke climbed into his Rockwell B-1 Lancer heavy bomber after briefing a group of other pilots. Often known as the "bone," for B-One, the aircraft is one of three heavy bombers that the Air Force currently uses. Burke commanded a wing of 30 Lancers preparing for a bombing run against the Bartholomew Martin compound in Erbil, Kurdistan. The wing was split into three groups of ten planes, each group assigned to specific targets on the Reformer compound.

"I have the target in sight," he said into his radio, which was picked up at the Situation Room in the White House as well as the Pentagon. "Commencing first run against the armored vehicle compound."

In successive sweeps, the bombers attacked the troop barracks, the munitions building, the armored vehicle area, and Bartholomew Martin's headquarters. After 10 minutes, the entire compound was a scene of smoking rubble.

"Any surprises to report, Jim?" General Dolan asked from his post at the Pentagon.

"Yes, sir, plenty of surprises. What I'm looking at is nothing that I expected. Reports from the other pilots confirm my observations. We didn't see any planes on the air strip, nor did we see any tanks in the armor staging area. Also, when we bombed the ammunition dump I expected to see a gigantic explosion. The only thing that apparently blew up were our own bombs. I didn't see any personnel running around either. I'm alerting the ground commander that he can commence his attack now. Something tells me he's not going encounter a hell of a lot of resistance."

A tank battalion, consisting of four platoons of 14 M1 Abrams battle tanks each, charged into the compound, followed by infantry units.

Brigadier General Bruce Harding, the officer in charge of the tank battalion, radioed what he saw to General Dolan at the Pentagon and to the White House Situation Room.

"A computer video war game is more violent than what I'm seeing, general. This place looks deserted. I can see no vehicles of any type, including tanks, trucks, and automobiles. I have yet to see any personnel. It looks to me like somebody heard we were coming and got out of here— fast. I'm dispatching minesweepers to look for IEDs and booby traps."

The President stood in the White House Situation Room, not liking what he heard. He turned to Dee and Jake.

"It looks like Bartholomew Martin has pulled off another vanishing act. The Reformers compound is empty."

"It's obvious," Dee said, "that Martin has his people imbedded throughout our government. He had plenty of warning about this attack. The son of a bitch may be without a title, but he's not without power."

"Dee, We knew this operation faced a chance of failure," the president said. "To pull this off I've had to negotiate with the Kurds, the Iraqis, the Turks, and countless other entities to make sure we didn't get into a battle with anybody other than Bartholomew Martin. Hell, we call the place Kurdistan, but it's really part of Iraq."

"Honey, I mean Mr. President, you've done everything you possibly could," Dee said, violating her personal rule not to call him anything but Mr. President.

"The First Lady's right, Mr. President," Jake Arnold said. "You've done your best, sir."

"Thanks for not calling me 'honey,' Jake." Sometimes it pays to lighten up.

"Our next mission is going to be even tougher than attacking a compound," the president said. "We now have to find that elusive bastard. It's obvious that he's up to something. And when Bartholomew Martin is up to something, it's big."

CHAPTER SIXTY FIVE

"I could get used to having our own private airplane. How about you, Bill?"

"I think I understand why they're treating us like royalty, hon. We may not like it, but we're the center of the entire investigation."

"Folks, it's now my job to make you two look ridiculous," the FBI agent said. "I have wigs for both of you and a beard for Bill. I guess you've figured out that we're worried about you. You can take these things off after you get into the car that's waiting at the airport."

The plane landed at Newark International Airport in New Jersey. As promised, a car was not only waiting, but was positioned on the tarmac.

"You're going to love where I'm taking you—a beautiful house in Tenafly, New Jersey."

"Why?" both Bill and Nancy asked.

"Secretary Bellamy himself will be there to tell you."

The car pulled into a long winding driveway of a house that the FBI agent had accurately described as beautiful. It stood two stories high on an acre of treed property. They both noticed that a fence surrounded the land in front of the trees. Bill noticed that there were security cameras on poles all over the property. The car pulled up to the rear door as they put on their disguises and got out.

"Welcome to your new home," I said as I met them at the door.

"Our new home?" they both said.

"Congratulations, you are now proud members of the FBI Witness Protection Program."

"Is this really necessary?" Nancy asked.

"Allow me to be blunt, Nancy," I said. "If I were an odds-maker I'd peg your chances of survival at zero if you weren't in the program. It hasn't hit the news yet, but we've just learned that Frank Morgan, the CEO of Rosetta Corporation, died in a car accident. The police reported that the accident was suspicious."

"Oh, my God," Nancy said. "Frank Morgan was a good man. Have they picked a successor as CEO?"

"Yes, they have. A gentleman known as Philip Duncan, who is—or was—an old college buddy of mine. We'll be talking about him at quite some length."

"That slimy fuck," Nancy said. "Pardon my Montana language."

"Morgan's car was sideswiped by a truck and smashed into a barrier," I continued. "We've seen this maneuver before. It's a long story, but that's how the president and first lady met. As a lawyer, he represented his future wife in a wrongful death lawsuit for the death of her husband. He was killed in a sideswipe collision that was later discovered to be a murder. The case has become famous in law enforcement and intelligence communities as '*The Sideswipe Conspiracy.*' That's how I met them. As the head of the FBI Joint Terrorism Task Force at the time, it was my pleasure to introduce them to the FBI Witness Protection Program. They still speak warmly of the experience. I'm happy to say that I was there when they got married on their second day in the program. I understand that you two are planning to marry, so why not have your wedding reception in this beautiful house. Just don't plan on too many guests. We'll save you some time and choose the guests for you."

"How long do you expect us to be in the program, Rick?" Bill asked.

"Can't say. We're starting to close in on what looks like a gigantic plot, and we'll need you two to help us sort it out and to testify in court if necessary. We'd prefer to kill the bastards, but assuming the cases go to trial, you will earn your benefits of the Witness Protection Program. Hey, let's have lunch and plan your wedding."

"Something tells me that our wedding plans have been simplified," Nancy said. "If I understand you correctly, you will pick the guests and we will agree. Or something like that."

"Exactly like that," Bellamy said. "My assistant, Sally Boynton, is an FBI agent. I'm sure she'll be happy to serve as your Maid of Honor, Nancy. I'll be honored to stand up as your Best Man, Bill. The person who will officiate is Father Walter Gentile, the Chaplain for Federal Plaza. He's an FBI agent as well as an Episcopal priest. My wife, Ellen, is also on the list. Although it isn't known publicly, she's a deputy FBI agent. Ellen's also my closest aide."

"Ellen Bellamy, the TV star?" Bill said.

"The one and only."

"You guys sound like you do this all the time," Nancy said.

"You got that right, Nancy. The Federal Bureau of Investigation—your perfect wedding planners. We even have a designated shopper who will be here this afternoon to take your shopping list for your new clothes. So, when shall we hold your wedding?"

"How about this coming Saturday?" Nancy said as she looked at Bill.

I dialed a number on my phone.

"Hi Father Walt, Bellamy here. How about a wedding at location Xray Zulu this Saturday at two? Great. I'll have a car pick you up."

Nancy and Bill said nothing. They just stared at me.

"I wish we could wrap up investigations as efficiently as we do weddings," I said. "Let's have lunch. This afternoon you two will tell us everything you know about the new CEO of the Rosetta Corporation."

CHAPTER SIXTY SIX

September 13

"*Moonwalker, Moonwalker*, this is Rosetta, come in please."

"This is *Moonwalker*, read you loud and clear, Rosetta. Astronaut David Hardy speaking. With me is astronaut Tim Jordan. We've run all tests this morning and I report AOK. *Moonwalker* is now fully operational.

"David, this is Phil Duncan. Are you ready for a full satellite test run? I want you to take it slow because this will be the first test without input from the former *Stargazer* astronauts Mullin and Cranston. They had to go to New York. Something about Mullin's grandmother being sick."

"Phil, Tim Jordan and I heard a rumor that Cranston and Mullin killed our astronauts who were supposed to take over *Stargazer*."

"Don't pay attention to rumors that don't concern you, David."

"Yes, sir. We're ready to start the tests."

"Starting with satellite one, begin the full test of each orbiter."

After they started the first satellite test, Hardy turned to Jordan.

"I could swear that I overheard Duncan himself say that Cranston and Mullin killed our guys."

"Hey, Dave, you know how Duncan gets pissed off when people ask too many questions, not to mention Bartholomew. I suggest we do our jobs and keep our well-paid mouths shut."

"Satellite tests are all positive, Rosetta. I'm commencing the solar panel tests."

The solar panel tests took another five minutes each, adding 100 minutes for the entire operation.

"The panels on satellite three are not responding, Rosetta. They are going through rotation sequences on their own, as expected." Hardy said.

"Attempt to use the override switch, David."

"It doesn't respond, Phil."

"Yes, I can see," Duncan said, smiling.

The mid-September temperature reading was 71 degrees Fahrenheit at the beginning of the test. It read 31 degrees by the end of the test. The clouds thickened, and snow flurries appeared.

The entire test operation was observed and recorded by a new satellite that had been launched by NASA two weeks before. Nancy and Bill Cranston, now married, sat in the mission control building at the Kennedy Space Center, taking a break from the FBI's beautiful safe-house in New Jersey. I was with them.

"Right on cue," Nancy said. "After the solar panels began rotating on satellite three, the panels on all of the satellites began to turn. We can see now that they are all angled toward the sun's rays, reflecting them back into space. Look out the window. I'm guessing snow."

"The temperature is 31 degrees and dropping," Bill said, looking at the weather app on his smartphone, "and yes, it's starting to snow. A beautiful September day here in Central Florida."

"That nails it," I said. "The new space station is Rosetta property and Nancy just called the shots as we saw them. Rosetta is the cause of our weather, and Philip Duncan is the prick behind it."

"But who's behind Duncan?" Bill Cranston asked.

"Bill, you're one of us now, but you don't have a 'need to know' the answer to your question at this time. You'll find out soon enough. Pardon me. I have to step into the next room and make a call to the White House."

***

"Mr. President, I've seen the smoking gun. Nancy Mullin walked us through what we were watching on the display for our new satellite. Of course, we couldn't see the switches being thrown, but we saw the solar panels on all satellites rearrange themselves. The temperature here is below freezing and the snow is getting heavy. Philip Duncan was calling the shots from Rosetta headquarters. I have enough to arrest him right now."

"Don't even think about it, Rick. I know it's tempting to nail a guy when you've got the evidence, but Duncan isn't our target, as you well know. He's just a functionary. Have you been briefed on the results of our operation in Kurdistan?"

"Yes, sir, I have. Bartholomew Martin obviously had a lot of warning before the attack. Do we know where they've moved?"

"We'll know shortly. Our senior guy at CIA is on top of the matter. Nobody gets away from him."

"Do you mean Buster, Mr. President?"

"Yes. As I said, shortly we'll know Bartholomew's new mailing address."

CHAPTER SIXTY SEVEN

September 14

"Exactly 142 miles southwest of Tehran, Mr. Director."

"Knock off the Mr. Director bullshit, Buster. Fill me in on the details."

"The people who pulled off the escape from Dunkirk in World War II should have had Bartholomew Martin in charge, Bill. Their compound in Kurdistan was stripped bare. They didn't even bother to leave IEDs or booby traps. They just got the hell out of there. My inside people tell me that they made a mad dash from Erbil to their present position in Iran in just under nine hours. They loaded their tanks onto flatbed trucks and hauled ass. The place where they've set up their new compound is an abandoned Iranian Army base. The area is so desolate it doesn't even have a name, but my guys think they're calling it by the English words *Reformation City*, typical of Bartholomew Martin. As you know, the Reformers are darlings of the ayatollahs because they both hate the United States, and they both want to do anything possible to screw us. A land attack through the Iranian countryside is impossible, to overstate the obvious. We blew our shot at nailing Bartholomew and his snakes in Kurdistan, so now we have to come up with alternatives, all of which are above my pay grade."

"No, it's not above your pay grade, Buster. You're the best spook in the CIA, and your thinking always goes beyond mere spying. You're a strategist, and don't give me humble pie crap by denying it."

"Well, there is a simple answer, Bill, but it's so simple it's stupid. We now know, thanks to Rick Bellamy and his people from Homeland Security, that the Rosetta Corporation is nothing more than a tool of Bartholomew Martin. Rick has been working with the two astronauts we rescued from *Stargazer* and we now have a microscope on the whole operation. Rosetta's *Stargazer* program became a technical means for Bartholomew to get control of the world's weather. The astronauts, Nancy Mullin and Bill Cranston, who are now Mr. and Mrs. Cranston, are heaven sent. They both narrowed their suspicions down to the former operations VP of Rosetta, a guy named Philip Duncan, an old college friend of Rick Bellamy if you can believe it. They observed the 20 satellites that are controlled by *Moonwalker*. Cranston and Mullin were the astronauts aboard *Stargazer* and are intimately familiar with the controls which are almost identical to *Moonwalker*."

"Hey, Buster, you just said that the answer was so simple it's stupid. So, my long-winded friend, what is the simple stupid answer?"

"We bust Rosetta and take over by court order."

"But that doesn't solve the long-range problem, which is Bartholomew Martin."

"That's why it's a stupid answer, Bill. That fucking megalomaniac will still be at large. Our country has some big problems on its plate—North Korea, Iran, and now Bartholomew and his Reformers, who are under the friendly wings of the Iranian mullahs. Do I have to remind you that Bartholomew is our most recent president? If it weren't for Matt Blake and his wonderful wife, we'd be living in a goddam dictatorship. So that's why stomping on Rosetta is only a short-term solution, which is a stupid answer."

"Buster, you're the smartest guy around here, which is why I keep you close so I can take credit for your brilliance. But don't you think that sometimes a short-term solution is a good one. Hey, it's mid-September and we're having ourselves another blizzard. At this moment, it wouldn't be an exaggeration to say that Bartholomew is in control of the world's weather, which means he's pretty much in control of the world. Put yourself in President Blake's shoes. He can't allow this dangerous weather to keep on happening. He knows that he's got to deal with Bartholomew. Hell, he recently tried to destroy the prick and his entire organization in Kurdistan. Buster, you're doing a great job of tracking what's going on with the Reformers. But somebody's got to plow this goddam snow."

"Well, there's even a simpler solution, which is even more stupid," Buster said. "We know for certain, thanks to the Cranstons, that the weather is being controlled from Rosetta, using *Moonwalker*, the newly launched space station. Why don't we simply blow up *Moonwalker*?"

"What? Yes, we know that the new space station controls the satellites, but even the Cranstons aren't sure how. If we blow the damn thing up, we could permanently change the weather with no way to reverse it. We don't know how they're doing it, but Bartholomew uses Duncan and his people to keep changing the weather to throw us off balance. It's as if they keep testing the thing to prepare for a major event. But one thing we do know is that Bartholomew Martin wants to control the weather. Hey, look out the window. The snow is letting up and the sun looks like it's about to come out. I have a hunch that Duncan, probably on orders from Martin, is backing off on the wild weather because he knows that the Cranstons have disappeared from Rosetta. I think they're trying to calm things down a bit, so we don't take any drastic steps. Let's get in touch with Rick Bellamy. He's at the Kennedy Space Center with our two favorite astronauts."

***

"Mr. Secretary, it's the Director of the CIA on the secure line for you, sir."

"Bellamy here. Go ahead, Bill."

"Rick, is the weather changing where you are?"

"Yes, it is," I said. "I'm with Bill and Nancy Cranston and we're monitoring what's going on with our new space station. Of course, we can't see the controls, but somebody has been hitting the buttons, this time giving us a break. I think they're intentionally backing off so we won't attack them."

"I agree, Rick. We have a lot of assets in place at Rosetta, deep cover assets as well as FBI agents in the open. I'm here with Buster, and he tells me we have 12 CIA people at Rosetta, posing as regular employees. As of right now we're almost certain, just based on the facts we know, that the space station operation, including the weather controls, is being handled from Rosetta, not Bartholomew Martin's new location in Iran. I think we need to meet with President Blake. We can only go so long in not putting a stop to Martin."

CHAPTER SIXTY EIGHT

September 15

President Blake took advantage of the moderating weather to call a meeting at the White House.

Those present were First Lady Dee, Rick and Ellen Bellamy, Bill Carlini and Buster from the CIA, and FBI Director Sarah Watson. Astronauts Bill and Nancy Cranston were there as well, on the president's specific orders.

"I think you will all agree that we can no longer put up with this unpredictable weather. For our entire country, actually the world, it's the equivalent of being under siege. Our entire infrastructure isn't designed for these wild weather swings. The Secretary of the Treasury gave me a report just how much this madness is costing our economy. The price tag could be as high as 10 trillion dollars over the next five years—that's *five years*. Blizzard conditions for a full week are enough to put a small business into bankruptcy, as well as the companies that supply them. And I remind you that small businesses are the backbone of our economy. The Justice Department tells me that bankruptcy filings are at a record high in courts across the country. Not only is our domestic economy taking a hit, but the global financial structure is hostage to this insanity as well. And it isn't just the economic impact, huge as it is, but the millions of choices and decisions that people make every day. I'm sure that our newlywed space heroes, Bill and Nancy Cranston, would prefer not to live out their lives in the Witness Protection Program."

The Cranstons smiled and nodded emphatically.

"We're here because of one man—Bartholomew Martin, the most ambitious tyrant since Adolf Hitler."

"Oh my God," Nancy said. "Do you mean the former President of the United States?"

"The one and only, Nancy," the President said. "Over the past few days our knowledge of where we stand has improved, and our choices have narrowed. We launched the biggest attack since World War II on Martin's compound in Kurdistan, only to find it empty. He and his thugs have now decamped to the land of one of our worst adversaries, Iran. To attack the compound near Tehran would be to enter a war, a gigantic war. But having said that, we know that Bartholomew Martin must be stopped. World peace never depended more on a single course of action. Everyone in this room has top-secret security clearance, including most recently, Bill and Nancy Cranston. We have to share ideas, because you people know more about this problem than the rest of our government. First Lady Dee suggested that we indulge in some good old-fashioned brainstorming, and I couldn't agree with her more, especially because we have so many brains in this room. We're going to go around the table and I want a one-word response from each of you, one word that you each think is a key to our going forward. I'll start with the two people at the end of the table, Bill and Nancy Cranston.

"Nancy?"

"Duncan."

"Bill?"

"Duncan."

"Rick Bellamy?"

"Duncan."

"Let me be a bit unorthodox and ask for a show of hands. How many people think the word Duncan is key to our next step?"

Everyone in the room raised their hand but Buster wanted to add something. When he raised his hand he said, "with an explanation."

"When the man who our CIA director calls 'super spook' has an explanation, I'd like to hear it."

"As you're aware, Mr. President," Buster said, "the CIA has some deeply imbedded spies at Rosetta. They've fed us a steady stream of information about Philip Duncan, but were it not for our astronaut friends, the Cranstons, it would be just a lot of unconnected dots. From what I've heard, when Bill and Nancy called Rick Bellamy and told him that Bill saw Duncan a few hours after *Stargazer* exploded and the man said nothing, Rick knew immediately that he had to get them into protective custody. Duncan's silence that morning was the dot that connected all the other dots. Rick was sharp enough to tell Nancy to make up a story about her sick grandmother, a woman who passed away many years ago. The purpose of that call was to throw Duncan off the scent of knowing that they were on to him. Whisking them away also saved their lives. But Duncan is a smart guy, and it's just a matter of time before he realizes that the government has him in the crosshairs."

"That's a great explanation, Buster, but do you have a recommendation about what action to take with the elusive Philip Duncan."

"One of my imbedded moles has a talent for voice impersonation," Buster said. "He's always a hit at parties. He'd show up and speak to the host for a couple of minutes and then do an impersonation of the host's voice that was perfect. A few minutes after I met the guy he did an imitation of me that made me think I was talking to myself. He's amazing. I bet he could get on the phone right now with Nancy or Bill, two people who know Duncan well, and they would think they were speaking to the man himself. He's also technically smart as hell, one of my best people. I recommend that we arrest Duncan and the four others we know are with him. Then, with the technical assistance of Bill and Nancy Cranston, my voice impersonation guy will talk to the Reformer astronauts, and even to Bartholomew Martin himself. So, we'll turn Rosetta into a weather-controlling entity staffed by our people. I haven't figured it out yet, but we can use my voice guy to lure Bartholomew out into the open."

"He may talk a lot, but Buster's the best damned spook on the planet," Bill Carlini said. "Buster, how about a demonstration. Call your impersonation guy and tell him to do a Duncan imitation on speaker phone."

Buster dialed a number from the secure phone.

"Bob Columbo, please."

"Bob, it's me. I'm in a meeting at the White House, and I'd like you to do an impersonation of Mr. X over the speaker phone. Bill and Nancy Mullin are here. Go ahead."

"Phil Duncan here wishing you all a pleasant day. To celebrate, I'm cooking up a blizzard for your traveling pleasure. Bill and Nancy, congratulations on your wedding. At least I didn't rain on your parade. This is Phil Duncan, signing off."

Anybody in the room who had ever spoken to Duncan cracked up laughing.

"He sounds exactly like Duncan," Nancy said, "not similar, but exactly. Here's an idea. We must have tons of voice tapes of Bartholomew Martin from the years he was president. Imagine a fake Martin calling Duncan and then Duncan returning the call to talk about what they had discussed."

"If you ever tire of being an astronaut, Nancy," Buster said, "you'd make a great spook."

"Buster, do we have a phone number where Bartholomew Martin can be reached?" Bill Carlini asked.

"Bartholomew's phone number is one of the secrets of the universe," Buster said.

"Okay, folks," President Blake said, "in a few hours we're going to pull off one of the most sensitive operations we've ever handled."

CHAPTER SIXTY NINE

FBI Agent Walter Drake was the senior agent at Rosetta headquarters. He had orders directly from FBI Director Watson to carry out a critical mission, and to accomplish it in five minutes.

"We have a list of four people to arrest," Drake said to his group of seven FBI agents. Our first task is to lure each of them to a location where their arrest won't be seen by witnesses. I've chosen the office of the CEO Philip Duncan, our primary target."

"How will we get them there?" one of his agents asked.

"Bob Colombo, one of the CIA guys here, is a talented voice impersonator. He'll call each of our targets, speaking in the voice of Duncan. The time to execute is set for 11:30 a.m. today, two hours from now. There is a corridor from the Duncan's office leading directly to a private parking space behind the building. The office was set up that way, so the top man could sneak in and out of his office without being seen. We'll escort them into a waiting van that will take them into custody. Once they're all off premises, FBI Agent Jack Foreman will take over and announce his position as interim CEO. President Blake has cleared this with the chairman of the board of Rosetta, who is a personal friend. We've been briefing Foreman for days. He's one of us, so we don't have to worry about giving him too much information. Each of you have your scripts to recite to any employee who asks if you know what happened. Again, just say that Duncan and the others went to a meeting and should return shortly. Consider Duncan's cell phone the most valuable piece of equipment in the entire building. I will grab it, but in case anything happens, make sure you get custody of that phone."

***

Buster sat in my office at 26 Federal Plaza in New York.

"It's time to make it happen, Buster."

Buster dialed Bob Colombo, his undercover voice impersonator.

"Bob, it's Buster. Okay, you're about to launch your first live action scene as the voice of Philip Duncan. You have the script and the phone numbers of the men to call. Make all the calls right after 11 a.m. and tell them to report to Duncan's office immediately, 11:30 at the latest. I don't expect any questions because they're accustomed to taking orders from Duncan. If any of them tries to say he can't make it, switch into the 'nasty Duncan' voice that you've rehearsed with Nancy and Bill Cranston. I don't see any problem getting them to Duncan's office. Walter Drake, the lead FBI guy, will let me know after the deal is sealed."

***

"What the hell are you doing in my office?" Duncan said to agent Walter Drake.

"Stand up with your hands in the air," Drake said. "You're under arrest for treason and other crimes you will find out about at your arraignment. You have the right to remain silent. Anything you say can and will be used against you in a court of law and may also result in my cracking your fucking skull open. Hand me your cell phone and sit behind your desk with your hands where I can see them. We're about to have an impromptu meeting with your colleagues."

As each man walked into Duncan's office, an agent immediately handcuffed him and read him his rights. Drake then cuffed Duncan and the group left the office, walking down the corridor to the waiting van. The van would take them to the airport to board a private jet to take them to Washington, where they would be jailed pending arraignment.

"Hi, Buster, it's Walter Drake. Secretary Bellamy and Director Watson told me to communicate directly with you. I'm happy to report that Duncan and his accomplices have been apprehended and are on their way to Washington. Jack Foreman has been thoroughly briefed as you know, and has taken over as interim CEO of Rosetta, although that fact has not been announced to anyone yet."

"Great job, Walter. It's always a pleasure working with FBI guys. Mission accomplished."

"Thanks. Hey, is your real name 'Buster?'"

"You'll never know, my friend. Pardon me while I disappear back into the shadows."

***

"*Moonwalker, Moonwalker*, this is Home Base, come in."

"Read you loud and clear, Home Base, astronaut David Hardy speaking."

"Good afternoon, David, Phil Duncan here," Bob Colombo said.

"We're cancelling the satellite tests scheduled for tomorrow, David. You and Mike Jordan can just perform your normal internal tests."

"Is everything okay, Mr. Duncan? Why are you cancelling the tests?"

Jordan looked at Hardy wide-eyed and punched him in the arm.

"If I want you to question decisions of senior management, I'll publicly announce your promotion. Until then, kindly obey orders," Duncan/Colombo said.

"Yes, sir, Mr. Duncan."

CHAPTER SEVENTY

"Please give me a full report on the American raid on our compound in Kurdistan, Douglas," Bartholomew Martin said to his assistant.

"To say that we caught them by surprise would be an understatement, Bartholomew. Your idea of the rapid evacuation and relocation turned out to be brilliant. The Americans began with bombing raids that were gigantic in scope and followed up with infantry attacks led by a tank battalion. The only result for the Americans was a loss of munitions."

"Any indication that the Americans know about our new home?"

"I'm sure they are aware of our new location, Bartholomew. We can assume that America has spies in Iran. It's impossible to conceal such a large movement of people and equipment. But the significant fact is that we managed to move *everything*, including tanks and other heavy weapons to our new location here at Reformation City. Because the Americans know that an attack on our compound would mean war with Iran, we are actually safer here than in Kurdistan."

"I wonder, Douglas, if the Iranians are aware of our control over the Rosetta space station and its satellites. What have you heard from any of the Iranian leaders about the cold spells we've been having?"

"They blame it on the Americans, Bartholomew, just as they blame almost any unpleasantness on them. But recently the weather has not been an issue at all because we reversed the solar arrays. Today's temperature is a perfect 70 degrees Fahrenheit, normal for September in this part of Iran."

"Have you heard anything about the Iranian reaction to the name we've chosen for our new location?"

"Yes, the high authorities in Iran like the name you've chosen. One of them told me that Reformation City sounds 'Islamic.'"

"To change the subject, Douglas, what do the Americans know about the new space station, *Moonwalker*?"

"As far as they know it is Rosetta Corporation's space station and was put into orbit according to a regular schedule. Philip Duncan has done a wonderful job in my opinion, of convincing the Americans that Rosetta is on their side."

"Anything to tell me about Frank Morgan, Rosetta's CEO?"

"As you know, Bartholomew, Frank Morgan died in an unfortunate car accident, and Phil Duncan was chosen by the board as his natural successor."

"Yes, indeed it was an unfortunate car accident," Bartholomew said, stifling a laugh. "Philip Duncan is a good man and has been our main insider at Rosetta for years. I will be speaking to him shortly. As always, and it won't change now that he's CEO, I will talk to him sparingly to avoid suspicion. Do you suggest anything I should ask him?"

"Isn't the new space station, *Moonwalker*, ready to perform satellite tests? Perhaps you should ask him if there is anything special that they should do. And also—what is the status of the two former *Stargazer* astronauts, William Cranston and Nancy Mullin? The last I heard was that they had to fly east suddenly because of Ms. Mullin's ailing grandmother. I believe that you were concerned about running tests without those two present to give technical advice."

"Yes, Douglas, good suggestion. Our new astronauts, Hardy and Jordan, ran a test a few days ago and it was quite sloppy. I will feel more comfortable if Cranston and Mullin are on the line giving them advice. Unless

Cranston and Mullin have returned, I think that Philip Duncan will want to postpone the tests. Stay here while I call him."

***

"Good afternoon, Philip. This is Bartholomew."

"Hello, Bart. Good to hear from you," Bob Colombo said, using his best Philip Duncan imitation. Research from the CIA and the FBI had confirmed that Duncan is the only person who refers to Bartholomew as "Bart."

"Philip, I recommend that we postpone our plans for the satellite tests for a few days. It's essential that Nancy Mullin and William Cranston, the astronauts who operated *Stargazer*, be present to help our new astronauts with the controls. The tests that Hardy and Jordan ran didn't work so well, as you know. The switch procedures are quite exacting, and experience is necessary. Where is Nancy Mullin, Phillip? Is she still visiting her grand-mother?"

"I believe she is, Bart. She left a message with me saying that her grand-mother was ill and that she and Bill Cranston went to New York to visit her."

"You *believe* she's still in New York? Philip, you are aware of the impor-tance of the satellite tests are you not? When did Mullin leave?"

"Five days ago, along with Cranston."

"Do you know what flight they took? I assume there are very few flights from Billings to New York."

"No, Bart, I didn't check but I will as soon as I get off the phone."

"I recommend, Philip, that you exercise more caution and suspicion when someone gives you an excuse for not following orders. I'm sure you have Ms. Mullin's cell phone number. Contact her now to find out when she and Cranston will return. I will call you tomorrow at 9 a.m. your time to see what you found out and to let me know when we can run the satel-lite tests."

***

"Buster, it's Bob Colombo. Bartholomew wants a report from me to-morrow as to when we can expect Nancy Mullin to return to Rosetta. He also wants me to check on the flight she and Bill Cranston took. Of course, we know that they took a private FBI flight to New York."

"Just have your assistants call the airline and check for the flight numbers around the time when Nancy supposedly went to visit her imaginary grandmother. Since Duncan and his colleagues are no longer there, it won't be a problem for Nancy and Bill to show up at Rosetta. Just to be safe, I'll send them with bodyguards. I want Nancy and Bill to conduct the satellite tests with the astronauts aboard *Moonwalker*. Bartholomew must be convinced that Nancy and Bill are back on the job, otherwise your cover is blown. Call me tomorrow after you speak to Bartholomew. Tell him that the tests are scheduled for the day after tomorrow. I'll call Rick Bellamy to make sure the Cranstons take one of our planes to Billings this afternoon so that they'll be there when Bartholomew calls you. My guess is that he'll want to speak to Nancy. Bob, always remember, Bartholomew Martin doesn't trust a soul."

"Buster, something has been nagging me. What if Bartholomew arranges for somebody to show up at Rosetta wanting to speak to Duncan? I can imitate his voice but not his appearance. Security is pretty tight at Rosetta and people can't just walk in and wander around, but what can the receptionist say if somebody asks for the guy who is not here?"

"Put two of our agents on a rotating schedule to sit at the reception desk and brief them on what to say."

CHAPTER SEVENTY ONE

"When I talk to you on the phone, Bob, I can't believe that you're not Phil Duncan," Nancy said. "You sound exactly like him."

"Thanks for your compliment on my acting ability. I had to think fast when Bartholomew called me. I repeated your story about visiting your sick grandmother. He'll be calling tomorrow to get an update on when we can do the satellite tests. I knew that you had to be here. Since Duncan and his friends have been arrested and taken into custody, we saw no reason why you couldn't be here. Congratulations on your wedding, by the way."

"Thanks, Bob. So, you want us to assist the new *Moonwalker* astronauts on a full satellite test."

"Yes, and I expect that Bartholomew will want to speak to you. That's why we flew you here. We couldn't come up with a story why you can't help with the satellite tests."

***

"Hello, Bart, Phil Duncan here," Colombo said. "We've scheduled the satellite test for tomorrow. Nancy Mullin and Bill Cranston have returned from New York, and they're ready to assist with the tests."

"Are they nearby, Philip?"

"Yes, they're down the hall."

"I want to talk to them. Tell them that I'm Frederick Smith, a securities analyst with Goldman Sachs, and that I have some questions."

"Phil, Nancy," Colombo said out loud over the speaker phone, "I have a Mr. Frederick Smith on the phone. Please come to my office." He handed her a note that read, "It's Bartholomew Martin on the phone. He's posing as a securities analyst with Goldman Sachs, and they're considering a substantial investment in Rosetta."

"Hello, Ms. Mullin and Mr. Cranston, Fred Smith here from Goldman Sachs. Phil Duncan said it would be alright if I asked you a few questions. First, let me say that I hope your grandmother is in good health, Ms. Mullin. Phil Duncan told me that you had to fly to New York to be with her. Is she okay?"

"Yes, she's improved quite a bit in the past couple of days" Nancy said as she rolled her eyes. "Thank you for asking."

"Now for a couple of questions, if you don't mind. At Goldman Sachs we like to be very cautious when making a sizeable investment. Do you know the two gentlemen who are in control of the space station *Moonwalker*?"

"We haven't met personally," Nancy said.

"I understand that you and Mr. Cranston will assist them on satellite tests tomorrow, is that right?"

"Yes, it is, Mr. Smith. We'll be coaching them and helping with the satellite controls from right here in Billings."

"Thank you very much folks for taking the time to chat with me. Now I would like to go over a few things with Mr. Duncan."

"You folks can go back to what you were doing," Duncan/Colombo said loudly before he hit the speaker off button.

"So, it looks like we're good to go for tomorrow, Philip," Martin said. "I'm glad they're back on the job. I will call you tomorrow after the tests so we can compare notes."

The following day would see a satellite test as never before.

CHAPTER SEVENTY TWO

"*Moonwalker, Moonwalker*, this is Home Base, come in."

"Read you loud and clear, Home Base. This is Dave Hardy. Am I speaking to Mr. Duncan?"

"You guys can call me Phil. Bill Cranston and Nancy Mullin are here with me. They're here with me to help you with the satellite tests."

"Hello, Dave, Nancy Cranst…I mean Mullin, here with Bill Cranston. We're going to go through a full test of the 20 satellites including tests of their retractable solar panels. Each of the satellite tests will take seven minutes for a total of 140 minutes. We'll then test the solar panels, which have given us some difficulty recently. That will add another 100 minutes to the operation. Are you guys ready?"

"We're ready, Nancy, testing satellite number one."

The satellite tests were done, and the crew prepared to test each of the solar panel arrays.

"When you get to the third solar panel test," Nancy said, "be prepared to hit the override switch. As far as we know the fail-safe mechanisms on 17 of the satellites are not functioning, so be prepared to hit the override.

It's identical to the one on *Stargazer,* except that the one on *Moonwalker* works. Let me know once you have identified the switch."

The first two satellite solar arrays went smoothly. The third malfunctioned as they expected.

"Okay, hit the override switch Dave."

"From my readout here," Bill Cranston said, "it looks like the override isn't working—or hasn't been thrown."

"Dave, please confirm that you have activated the override switch," Nancy said. "Dave, can you hear me?"

"Yes, I can hear you, Nancy. We've been ordered not to throw the override switch."

"Ordered by whom?" Duncan/Colombo asked.

"I'm sure you know the answer to that question, Mr. Duncan," Hardy said. "The satellite solar arrays are now on their own."

The panels on each of 17 satellites slowly turned toward the sun, reflecting its warming rays away from earth and into space. The temperature in Billings went from 65 degrees Fahrenheit to 35 degrees in ten minutes. The skies darkened, silently announcing an approaching snow storm.

"The temperature here is now 35 degrees," Nancy said. "It's essential that you hit the override switch, or we'll soon be in the middle of a blizzard."

"I have my orders, Nancy," Hardy said.

"I spoke to the person who you said gave the orders," Duncan/Colombo said. "He mentioned nothing about the maneuver you've activated. I'm the CEO of this company and I'm ordering you to reverse the solar panels now."

"No can do, Mr. Duncan," Hardy said.

"Bob," Nancy said to Colombo after she turned the voice transmission switch off. "Why can't you call Bartholomew and see what you can find out."

"I guess nobody told you Nancy," Colombo said. "No one has Bartholomew's number, not even Duncan as far as we know. We have no way of contacting him, not that it would do much good anyway. He's going to do what he wants to do and fuck the rest of the world."

"But can't you impersonate Martin, Bob? I heard you do it once and your imitation was as good as your Duncan act."

"It won't work, Nancy. Bartholomew Martin has communicated with those astronauts and if they ask a question about a prior conversation with him I wouldn't know what to say. Besides, they would identify Duncan or Rosetta from caller ID."

***

"Al Roker here for *NBC Weather.* You don't need me to tell you what's happening. We're being socked with yet another arctic cold blast and snowstorm. The temperature outside our studio is 19 degrees, having fallen 41 degrees in 10 minutes. Prepare for another blizzard folks, a mid-September blizzard."

***

"Bellamy here, Mr. President. To put it bluntly, sir, none of us thought this could happen because of the recent actions we took at Rosetta."

"Rick, how the hell can this happen even if Duncan and his men are in custody? We removed the bad actors. What more can we do?"

"Mr. President, somebody near Tehran is calling the shots, I'm afraid. Bartholomew Martin was never directly involved in manipulating the satellites, but I believe he is now. Our guy at Rosetta said that the astronauts on *Moonwalker* flatly refused commands to override the solar panel deployment. The astronaut, a guy named David Hardy, said, and I quote. 'I have my orders.' Bob Colombo, our Duncan impersonator, told me that the astronaut said that he, Duncan, knew who was giving the orders. As of right now, sir, we have absolutely no control over the situation. We can only hope that Nancy and Bill Cranston can figure something out."

CHAPTER SEVENTY THREE

"The Iranian authorities are extremely upset, Bartholomew," Douglas Merriman said. "It's 19 degrees when it should be around 70. It's snowing heavily and they have no idea what to do about it. Snow removal is foreign to them."

"No problem, Douglas, they have absolutely no idea that we have anything to do with Rosetta, or its satellites, or the weather."

"Are we going to moderate the weather as we've done in the past?" Merriman said.

"No, Douglas. This time I want to show the world exactly what the Reformers can do. I'm going to let it snow for quite a while. Power is real when it's used, and I'm using it now. How are our people on the compound faring?"

"We have tanks with snow plow equipment, so the roads aren't a problem. The buildings are equipped with generators and heavy-duty heating units, which you ordered before we came here. Because we know what to expect, we're in a better position to handle the weather than anybody."

***

"This call is for you, Bob" Colombo's assistant said. "I think it's Bartholomew Martin. Better switch into Phil Duncan mode."

"Phil Duncan here, Bart. Judging from the weather, it seems that our new astronauts weren't successful with the solar panel override switch. We're in the middle of a blizzard here in Billings." Nancy stood next to Colombo scratching notes for him. "As you may be aware, Bart, we can stop this wild weather by reversing our satellite tests. Shall I contact *Moonwalker* and make that happen?"

"No, Philip, I want this weather to continue for a while. The timing will be by my discretion. Our astronauts have performed according to my orders. They're good men and know how to obey orders. There will be no satellite manipulation without my express order. Is that okay with you, Phillip?"

"Sure thing, Bart. I was just wondering how long this will continue. I think a lot of people are wondering the same thing."

"It will continue until I announce otherwise, Philip."

Martin lit a cigar after he got off the phone. He laughed out loud. *It will continue until I announce otherwise*, he thought.

CHAPTER SEVENTY FOUR

"I need to meet with my senior advisor," President Blake said.

"You mean Jerry Langdon at State?"

"No, Dee, I mean you. Anytime I've ever found myself in a box that I couldn't get out of, you're always the one who comes up with the answer. So, want to take a guess what kind of box I find myself in?"

"The entire country is in the same box as you, honey. Yes, I know what it is. Even though we've arrested Duncan and his men at Rosetta, we still have no control because the astronauts on *Moonwalker* answer only to Bartholomew Martin. Hell, we were lucky enough that Buster had that voice impersonation guy. But we're still out in the cold, not to pun."

"You summarized it precisely, babe. We control the Rosetta Corporation, but not the space station—Bartholomew does. Our CIA mole, Bob Colombo, the voice guy, tells us that Bartholomew said he intends to continue our current blizzard conditions indefinitely. So, don't let your brain take a rest now. How can we get out of this box?"

"This is going to sound insane, Matt, but we have to talk to the Iranians. I'm sure they don't know that their guests, Bartholomew and the

Reformers, are behind this weather. Iran is a country with a mild climate. They must be going nuts with freezing temperatures and a blizzard even more than us. Their agricultural output sucks because so much of the soil is sandy. Add some freezing temperatures to that problem and you've got a lot of hungry Persians. We must have some spooks imbedded in Iran who can get us to the leadership. Who are you calling?"

"Bill Carlini at CIA. We need to meet with him and his super spook, Buster. Have I mentioned lately, Dee, that you're a genius?"

***

Bill Carlini and Buster arrived at the Oval Office in a half hour.

"Dee has come up with a recommendation that's kind of bold, to say the least, and I want to pass it by you. Depending on what you tell us will determine whether we can do it or not. Dee, fill these guys in on your idea."

"As we all know, we're at a stalemate with Bartholomew Martin," Dee said. "From his new location, he probably thinks he's untouchable, and he just may be right. We can't storm into Iran like we did in Kurdistan because it would mean an all-out war. But we do have a set of facts on our side. The latest temperature plunge is hitting Iran more than most countries. Because of poor soil and lack of adequate water, Iran struggles to raise crops, even in the best of times. Intelligence reports tell us that the winter blasts this summer almost crippled Iran's farming output. The leadership invited Martin and his thugs to set up shop in Iran for a simple and familiar reason, their hatred of the United States, the Great Satan. But the simple facts tell us that the Iranian leadership doesn't know Bartholomew Martin is behind the cataclysmic weather. If they did, I think they'd view the Reformer compound as an enemy, not an ally. But the way to leak that information must come from somebody other than my husband because they'd never believe him. It's got to come from somebody inside. So that's what we want to talk about. Who are our spies in Iran, and especially, which one can speak to the Iranian high command?"

"Ramin Abbasi is the guy to pull this off," Buster said without hesitation. "He's an economist, a financial expert, and a mid-level minister. And he's all ours, as good a mole as we have. The mullahs rely on his advice because their tightly controlled economy is always a mess."

"I recall you telling me about this guy before," the President said. "Can he leak the word to the top without getting his head removed?"

"The reason Abbasi is such a great asset, Mr. President, is that the Iranians think that he spies on *us*. He fills them in with a steady supply of information about the United States, but nothing that you couldn't find in American newspapers. I give him a few tidbits every now to keep his cover on tight. All he needs to do is say that his inside American sources tell him that Bartholomew Martin and his group are the ones controlling the weather. He has the ear of Hamid Rashadi, a powerful mullah about three steps away from the top. Rashadi holds the title Deputy Foreign Minister. You would never know it from his words to the press, but Rashadi is one of the few true moderates in the regime, and we believe that he trusts Ramin Abbasi completely. Once they're convinced that Bartholomew and friends are the weather warriors they'll bomb the living shit out of them, pardon my Farsi."

"Honey, I mean Mr. President, I think we should turn Buster loose," Dee said. "I don't see any other way out of this mess. We need to get the Iranians on our side, not that they'll realize it."

"I agree. What do you think, Bill?"

"I've mentioned this to you in the past, Mr. President, but when I'm no longer in office, I couldn't recommend a better replacement for me than Buster. I've learned to trust his instincts over the years, and I agree with the First Lady that we should turn him loose. By the way, Dee, your idea is brilliant, simply *brilliant*."

"Okay, Buster," the President said. "It's time for you to let your friend Abassi in on one of our top secrets. Just tell him the truth—that we've recently discovered that Bartholomew Martin is controlling the weather through his planted insiders at Rosetta. Tell him all about the assassination of Rosetta CEO Morgan, and how we discovered that Duncan is Martin's hand-picked manager for controlling the world's weather. Give him all the details he asks for. Buster, it's time to work your spook magic."

CHAPTER SEVENTY FIVE

Deputy Foreign Minister Hamid Rashadi stood by the window in his office looking out at the gathering blizzard. Seventy degrees Fahrenheit would be a normal temperature in Tehran in the month of September, but his city was blanketed in snow and bitterly cold at 19 degrees. He wore a heavy sweater and a scarf. Although his office was heated, the system was designed for brief winter chills, not below freezing temperatures.

"Minister Ramin Abbasi is here for his appointment with you, sir," Rashadi's assistant said. Rashadi quickly walked to the door and opened it.

"It's wonderful to see you, my friend," he said as he wrapped Abbasi in a bear hug. "It's been too long. In our brief phone conversation, you said that you had some information about this damnable weather. Please have a seat while my assistant brings us some tea—hot tea."

His assistant walked in with a tray of tea and fruit snacks. Rashadi opened the drawer under the coffee table and pulled out a bottle of French Cognac.

"One of the many secrets you and I keep," Rashadi said as he poured

Cognac into Abbasi's cup. "So, tell me Ramin, what are your thoughts on the weather, and please don't tell me that it's snowing."

Abbasi chuckled at Rashadi's wisecrack.

"As you know, my friend," Rashadi continued before Abbasi could respond, "this godforsaken weather is destroying our country. Not only is it killing our crops, but it's ruining our economy because the snowdrifts prevent us from conducting normal commerce. And people are dying because there's no way for them to get to a hospital in an emergency. Never did we think to store snow-plowing equipment because we thought we would never need it. Your message said that you had something urgent to talk to me about, Ramin. Don't keep your old friend waiting. What is it?"

"Hamid, I think I just may have the most important intelligence I've ever gathered. I found this out on my recent trip to the United Nations in New York. Sometimes the Americans can be completely open with their loose lips. It concerns our guests a few miles from here, Bartholomew Martin, the former President of the United States, and his group, the Reformers."

"Whenever you visit the United States, Ramin, you come back with wonderful information. So, what did you find out about Bartholomew Martin and his group?"

"Hamid, you may want to take another sip of Cognac before I tell you what I've learned. To get right to the point, I have solid evidence, based on many conversations with the talkative Americans, that Bartholomew Martin is controlling the weather. Yes, the speculation that the weather is caused by an intentional act is true."

"Dear God, Ramin, how can that be true? How can Bartholomew Martin control the weather from a desolate region of our country?"

"He doesn't control it from here, but from the American West, a place called Billings, Montana, the city where the huge Rosetta Corporation is located. Rosetta owns and controls *Moonwalker*, the American space station, and an array of 20 satellites with solar panels. Martin controls the weather by rotating the panels to direct the sun's rays back into space, plunging the earth into a deep freeze along with snow. Martin arranged for the assassination of Mr. Frank Morgan, the founder and CEO of Rosetta. In Morgan's place he arranged for the elevation to CEO of Phillip Duncan, a former vice president of the company. Duncan is a stooge in Martin's pocket, and is one of his key allies, if not his most key ally. You will recall, Hamid, that *Stargazer*, Rosetta's space station before *Moonwalker*, was destroyed. The new space station is manned by two astronauts who are in the employ of Bartholomew Martin."

Rashadi stared at his friend wide-eyed. He poured them both another splash of Cognac.

"And the Americans are aware of this? Why haven't they put a stop to it? The horrible weather impacts North America just like the rest of the world. It's hard to imagine that the American government would tolerate something that occurs within its own borders."

"They did try to use force to stop them, Hamid. You will recall that the Americans launched a gigantic military operation against the Reformer compound in Kurdistan. They started with saturation bombing runs reminiscent of World War II. After bombing every inch of the compound, they launched an armor-led infantry attack. But, as we know, they found the compound empty. The Reformers made a daring high-speed escape to Iran after securing our permission. Martin wisely thought that his group would be safe within the borders of America's enemy." "As you know, Ramin, and of course what I'm about to say remains between us, but I have long thought that we picked the wrong enemy. The Americans may be clumsy bullies at times, but the Great Satan can also be a great friend. Instead, we support Islamic terror around the world. And now we give harbor to Bartholomew Martin and his group of mad men, for the only reason that he is an enemy of the United States. This is insanity, Ramin."

"Yes, Hamid, it is insane, and now we have a new piece of insanity to deal with—Bartholomew Martin's control of the weather. In one of the few times in history, Iran and the United States share a common enemy."

"My friend, I always value your wisdom and ideas. What do you propose we do with our dangerous guests?"

"I recommend a direct approach, Hamid. We should arrange for an emissary, perhaps yourself, to meet with Bartholomew Martin personally, and let him know that we've discovered his weather secrets. Order, not request, but order him to manipulate the satellites to reverse the destructive weather. Our country, with its small agricultural output, cannot tolerate having our few crops destroyed by freezing temperatures."

"How do you think Martin will react, Ramin?"

"I suggest that we control his reaction with an ultimatum. Either he reverses the satellites, or we will destroy him and his followers. Because his compound is in a desolate area of our country, you may want to suggest that we will drop a nuclear weapon on his compound. He doesn't know that we have yet to produce a nuclear bomb."

"I'm going to make an appointment to speak to Supreme Leader Khamenei. It won't be easy. His religious fanaticism often clouds his judgment. I'm sure he will resist the idea of attacking an enemy of the United States. I must impress upon him that Bartholomew Martin is as much our enemy as he is an enemy of the Americans. Khamenei loves intrigue and imagines himself a clever negotiator. Maybe I should suggest to him that we can use our actions as leverage to convince the United States to remove the crippling sanctions against us."

"Do you think the Supreme Leader will want the Americans to renew the nuclear weapons accord so we can develop our nuclear capability?" Abbasi said.

"Allah forbid he take such a ridiculous stance. President Blake is, in my opinion, not only a good and honorable man, but a ruthless leader when he wants to be. I think that Blake will chose to attack Martin's compound, therefore declaring war with Iran, rather than allow us to build a nuclear weapon. You and I know, Ramin, that a war with America will mean the end of Iran. If only Khamenei would admit that to himself."

"Like you, Hamid, I'm not an overly religious man, but I pray to Allah that someday we will see you as the leader of our country."

"Let's us not get ahead of ourselves, Ramin. I'm going to make an appointment to see the Supreme Leader, and I want you with me to answer his questions. We need to move fast. Each day of this imposed winter plunges us further into darkness."

CHAPTER SEVENTY SIX

"Mr. Bartholomew Martin is here for his appointment with you, Minister Rashadi."

"So, we're about to squeeze the trigger, Ramin. This will be the most important meeting you and I have ever held."

"Have a seat, Mr. Martin," Rashadi said.

"Please honor me by calling me Bartholomew."

"I shall call you Mr. Martin. I call friends by their first names, and I'm not certain you fit into that category. Let me get right to the point. I have irrefutable evidence that you and your organization are not only involved with our weather system but have direct control over it through the Rosetta Corporation in America."

"I have no idea what you're talking about, Mr. Deputy Minister. My organization, the Reformers, have taken you up on your hospitality so that we are free from interference by our mutual enemy, the United States. We are impacted by this strange weather just as everyone else."

"Mr. Martin, because you are American by birth, let me use a word that I'm sure you're familiar with—bullshit. You have imbedded two of your people as astronauts on the space station *Moonwalker,* taking directions from your insider at the Rosetta Corporation. We are aware that you have manipulated the Rosetta satellites and are controlling the weather. I had considered giving you an ultimatum, but instead I shall give you a command—order the satellite configuration to be reversed and return the earth to normal weather. I give you this command with the full cooperation of the United States government. If you do not take this action, we shall destroy your entire compound in Iran. If necessary we will use one of our nuclear bombs, without fear because you are in a desolate area of the countryside. You will act on my command *immediately*, using the telephone in front of you. Your cooperation is critical because the astronauts on the space station answer only to you. You are to speak to a Mr. Philip Duncan, Rosetta's president, and convey my command to him. Here is the phone, sir."

"But Mr. Deputy Foreign Minister…"

"The word 'but' has no place in this conversation, Mr. Martin. I did not give you a request or a suggestion, I gave you a simple command. Carry out the command or you will be placed under arrest and I shall order an immediate attack on your compound. Again, here is the phone."

"Philip, this is Bartholomew (speaking to Bob Colombo). I want you to do a satellite test run and reverse the solar panels to return the weather to normal."

"The last time I spoke to the astronauts they told me that they take orders from you and you only," Duncan/Colombo said. "If necessary, I will place you in communication with *Moonwalker* and you can give the command to follow my orders. Astronauts Cranston and Mullin are here with me and can walk the men on *Moonwalker* through the steps."

"Do it *now*, Mr. Martin," Rashadi said.

"*Moonwalker, Moonwalker*, this is Home Base, come in."

"Read you, Home Base. This is astronaut David Hardy. Is this Mr. Duncan?"

"Yes, it is," Duncan/Colombo said. "We're going to reverse the position of the satellites by rotating the solar panels and return the weather to normal. Any questions?"

"Mr. Duncan, the last time we spoke I told you that we only take orders from one man and it's not you."

"You have been taking orders from Bartholomew Martin. I will now patch you into him and let him give you the direct order."

"But but, how do I know it's Bartholomew Martin," Hardy stammered. "By the way, his name is not for disclosure."

"This is Bartholomew, David. Do as Mr. Duncan says immediately."

"Yes, sir, I mean Bartholomew."

"This is Nancy Mullin." She almost said Nancy Cranston. "Prepare to start the satellite sequence. Begin with satellite number one now."

They went through the satellite test and solar panel sequence taking 240 minutes as always. Minister Rashadi looked out the window and noticed that the snow had stopped, and the temperature according to a thermometer outside his window read 65 degrees Fahrenheit, normal for Tehran in September.

***

"You will now return to the compound that you call Reformation City," Rashadi said. "You will be brought there in an Iranian government vehicle, and you will be under armed guard. The Reformers are no longer the guests of the government of Iran. You will be under arrest and guarded the entire time it takes you to leave. Your tanks, planes, weapons, and other military impedimenta will become the property of the Iranian government. Good day, Mr. Martin."

CHAPTER SEVENTY SEVEN

"Agent Atkins is here for his appointment, Mr. President," his assistant said.

Dee was with the president in the Oval Office.

"Mr. President," Buster said, "when I told you that Ramin Abbasi was a valuable mole, I was making an understatement. I think we may have a deal with Iran that will be the end of Bartholomew Martin. Abbasi met with his close contact, Deputy Foreign Minister Hamid Rashadi, and told him all about Bartholomew Martin and his weather making. He sold Rashadi on the idea of Iran giving Bartholomew an ultimatum. The two of them then went to see Supreme Leader Khamenei."

"Let me guess that Khamenei, the maniac, wants us to renew the nuclear weapons accord," I said.

"That's why I think Abbasi is such a valuable insider, Mr. President. He and Rashadi managed to convince Khamenei that they need to move against the Reformers. They convinced him that Bartholomew Martin and his people are as much an enemy of Iran as they are of the United States, an even bigger enemy because the freezing weather is destroying the few crops that Iran produces. So, here's the offer. We immediately remove all sanctions against Iran, agree to purchase 50 billion American dollars' worth of Iranian bonds, and unfreeze the Iranian assets in the United States. And here's the best part—a renewal of the nuclear arms deal is off the table. They're willing to stop their nuclear development, and even agreed to allow inspectors onsite. Deputy Foreign Minister Rashadi can be here tomorrow to sign the agreement. They want to move fast because the freezing weather is killing them."

"Oh, my God," Dee said. "This is even more than I hoped for."

"Okay, let's make this happen fast," the President said. "I will personally meet with Rashadi along with Secretary of State Langdon. I want to nail this thing down before Khamenei comes up with some new ideas. Needless to say, I want an absolute, and I mean *absolute*, press blackout."

"You know me, Mr. President. The only member of the press I speak to is the paper boy."

CHAPTER SEVENTY EIGHT

"Good afternoon, ladies and gentlemen and welcome to a special edition of *The Ellen Bellamy Show*. With me today is Jerome Langdon, better known as Jerry, our Secretary of State. Mr. Secretary, I understand that you have some historic news to share with us this afternoon."

"Historic is the perfect word, Ellen. Yesterday afternoon, a treaty was signed in the Oval Office and was immediately confirmed by the senate in a voice vote, an historic first. The treaty hopefully will bring an end to the illicit reign of Bartholomew Martin, the former President of the United States. It's become a matter of public record recently that Bartholomew Martin and his large gang escaped from their compound in Kurdistan and created a new city in Iran, with permission of the Iranian government. Soon the Iranians learned that Martin and his followers, called the Reformers, were not the kind of guests they wished to entertain on their country's soil. As we all know, our country along with the rest of the world, has been subject to multiple spells of horrible freezing summer temperatures, along with record-setting blizzards. Iran, a country of moderate weather with temperatures that seldom go below freezing, was plunged into the frigid darkness along with the rest of us. Iran was especially impacted because of its modest farming output that became crippled with the freezing temperatures. Ellen, I've watched many of your shows about the weather. You interviewed guest after guest who tried to explain the weather and the climate. Some experts blamed it on climate change, others on shifting weather patterns. One thing that all the experts agreed on was that they really didn't know what was happening, other than to conclude that it was a natural phenomenon. We've recently learned that it wasn't natural at all, but a sinister manipulation of satellite solar panels that redirected the sun's rays away from earth and into space, creating winter in summer. None other than Bartholomew Martin, the totalitarian thug who was once our country's president, was the man behind it. When Tehran learned of Martin's activities we were all in the middle of one of his blizzards. The Iranians placed Martin under arrest and seized his group's assets. They are in the process of leaving Iranian soil, but Martin is still under armed custody."

"And how is our relationship with Iran, Mr. Secretary?"

"For the first time since the Iranian Revolution of 1979, our countries have conducted talks and reached an agreement that can only be described as cordial and mutually beneficial. The Iranians didn't need our agreement to arrest Bartholomew Martin, but both our countries agreed to cooperate on many levels. The most significant news about the talks is that Iran did not insist on continuing its nuclear program. We have lifted all sanctions and also agreed to economic assistance, but the nukes are off the table."

"Getting back to a subject I have come to hate, Mr. Secretary—the weather, what can you tell us?"

"We have received the full cooperation of the Rosetta Corporation, the company that owns the space station *Moonwalker,* which controls the satellites. Although senior management at Rosetta was unaware of it, Bartholomew Martin was controlling the satellites through *Stargazer* and then through *Moonwalker* from Rosetta headquarters using his inside hired henchmen. The two American astronauts who once controlled *Stargazer,* the station that was destroyed, assisted the current crew in positioning the satellites to enable earth's temperatures to return to normal. Today is September 25, and the temperature here in New York City is 72 degrees Fahrenheit, normal for this time of year. I'm sure you'll have an expert on your show soon who can explain exactly how the satellites changed our weather, somebody who can explain it better than I can."

"You're right, Mr. Secretary" Ellen said. "I'm sure I'll be interviewing experts, but I think you did an excellent job of explaining it. Can you tell us anything about the current situation with Bartholomew Martin? We all know that he had a taste of being a dictator when he was President of the United States, and recently focused on becoming dictator of the world through climate blackmail."

"Bartholomew Martin is under arrest and is imprisoned somewhere in Tehran. Because he committed his most recent crimes in Iran, and because he and his group were residents of Iran at the time, the Iranian government has legal jurisdiction to bring him to trial. An interesting development, an *extremely* interesting development, is that the Iranian government has asked for American assistance in prosecuting the case against Martin. It's been a long time since we've seen such cooperation between our two countries."

"So, there you have it ladies and gentlemen," Ellen said. "Our insane weather has come to an end and two old rivals are not only in conversation but are cooperating with each other. Sometimes I'm blessed with good news to cover, and this show has been one of those times. Folks, if you can, get outside and enjoy this beautiful September weather. That's what I'm going to do after the show."

***

"Rick is on line one for you, Ellen."

"So, what did you think of my happy show, hon?" Ellen said as she removed her earpiece.

"I'm not paid to be happy but to be a cynical nag, babe. But we should enjoy some happy times while we can. Let's go for a walk in the park. My Secret Service guys could use some exercise."

"And it will help prepare you for the next crisis."

"You know me too well, honey."

CHAPTER SEVENTY NINE

"Deputy Foreign Minister Rashadi is here, Mr. President. I'll escort him in."

Rashadi hated to wear the traditional flowing robes of Iranian big shots. He was dressed in an expensive Armani suit, making him look like an investment banker.

"It's good to see you again, Minister Rashadi," the President said.

"Please call me 'Hank,' Mr. President. "It's the name I answered to when I went to Northwestern University."

"I have a great memory, Hank. I believe you and I were at Northwestern at the same time. I recall you wearing the traditional robes of your country. Could that have been you?"

"I was a mullah-in-training. Little did my colleagues realize that I was becoming Westernized as well."

"Do you see us as the Great Satan, Hank?"

"Bullshit is bullshit, no matter what language it's in, Mr. President. I'm one of many Iranian officials—and I mean many—who look to the day when our countries can be friends and allies. My friend, Ramin Abbasi, is a mid-level government minister. He's the guy who called my attention to Bartholomew Martin. Frankly, I think Ramin is a CIA spy and that's fine by me. If you've got more spies like Hamid, keep them coming. He's a good man, and the world owes him its gratitude. Besides taking down that beast Martin, I think there's an even more positive outcome to this event. I'm hoping the Great Satan will be replaced by the Great Friend."

"I share that hope, Hank. I assume you don't drink, but can I offer you some tea or coffee?"

"We have been assuming too many things about each other since 1979, Mr. President. I'll have Kentucky bourbon, neat, three fingers, if you have it. Will you join me?"

"I long ago gave up drinking, Hank, but I'll raise my Diet Coke in toast—to our new friends."

"To our new friends, Mr. President. But let's not get ahead of ourselves. There are officials in my government and yours who don't share our warm feelings."

"What are Supreme Leader Khamenei's thoughts, Hank?"

"I expect that what I say won't be made public, Mr. President."

"Count on it, Hank. Your words will never leave this room."

"Thank you. I don't think I'd look good without my head. In answer to your question, Khamenei is an old-school Islamic fanatic. He actually believes all the nonsense that radical clerics like to spout. I negotiated with him after Ramin Abbasi told me about Bartholomew Martin. He finally agreed. I was certain that you and your government would not consent to reopen the nuclear pact talks. I finally managed to convince him to agree to the terms we signed. It may be an indication that he's mellowing, but I wouldn't count on it. For him to think about the United States in positive terms would go against his deeply ingrained principles. He may be the Supreme Leader by title, if not in fact. There are a number of people in our government, like me, who see America as a potential friend."

"It's a constant mystery to me, Hank, why Islam hates the West so much. Whether it's the Sunnis or the Shiites as in Iran, there is this hatred that many of us Westerners can't fathom."

"Mr. President, I'm going to let you in on a secret. If this ever becomes public I will be a dead man. I tell you this as a symbol of trust and our new friendship, because I'm putting my life in your hands. I'm a Christian, an Episcopalian. I converted, quietly, about five years ago. I was introduced to the words of Jesus Christ by an American diplomat. There's something about loving your fellow man that appeals to me more than murdering him because he's of a different religion. Thank God for the Internet, because I'm able to attend services online. This morning, wearing a disguise, I went to Mass and received communion. I was impressed by the priest's sermon. His name is Father Rick Sampson and he leads a parish here in New York. I'll never forget his words—'When things get tough, leave it to Jesus. He can figure it out better than us.' As our two countries slowly get to know one another, I'm going to repeat those words—to myself of course."

"Hank, as I once heard in a wonderful movie, 'I think this is the beginning of a beautiful friendship.'"

"You do a good Bogart, Mr. President."

CHAPTER EIGHTY EIGHT

"Good morning, Mr. Atkins," Hamid Rashadi said. "Please call me Buster, everyone else does."

"President Blake told me quite a bit about you, Buster. He's quite a fan of yours. And please call me Hank."

"He also told me quite a bit about you, Hank. We don't have too many Iranian friends, and you may be the best."

"Are you ready to visit Bartholomew Martin, Buster?" Rashadi said. "Your knowledge of this bastard will help us to prosecute him. He won't say a word to me."

"He's the most miserable scumbag ever to inhabit my country, pardon my Arabic. That one man came close to turning America into a dictatorship. With him as president we came close to earning the title Great Satan."

"Does he know you well, Buster?"

"Very well. When he was in the White House he tried to recruit me to spy on American politicians. He liked my background in intelligence with the CIA and wanted to use me to help him roll up our democracy."

"From what I heard about him, I'm surprised that he didn't arrest you when you refused to cooperate."

"The only reason I'm alive is that I didn't refuse. I made him *think* that I was his spy, but it was a big act. I spied on *him* and fed information to the growing opposition. I thank God that Matt Blake, President Blake, beat him in the election. Make no doubt about it, Hank, President Blake is a great man, and just what we needed after Martin's presidency."

"So, let's go to see the Reformer himself," Rashadi said.

Three jail guards led them down a long corridor to Martin's cell. One of the guards unlocked the door with his keys, as the other two stood by with their guns drawn, facing toward the cell.

"Buster, I think you know our guest," Rashadi said as he gestured toward the back of the cell. "I'll wait outside while you talk to him."

"Hank," Buster yelled as he stepped back into the corridor. "This cell is empty. Where's Martin?"

The guards rushed into the cell, guns drawn. They flipped the bed upside down and looked into every corner of the room. Bartholomew Martin was gone.

***

"Honey, your secretary just gave me this envelope addressed to me," Dee said. "Inside is another one addressed to you. I think somebody's playing games."

President Blake read the letter silently, and then looked at Dee. He was about to read it aloud when the intercom sounded.

"Mr. President, it's Buster on the line for you. He says it's urgent."

"Mr. President, Martin has escaped," Buster said. He was speaking from his cell phone in the corridor outside of Martin's cell. "This is the most secure prison in a land of secure prisons. Obviously, he had some help. The bastard is simply not here."

"His timing," the President said, "is typical of him. I just received a letter from him that was delivered to Dee. I was about to read it when you called. I'll read it now to you and Dee."

So, Mr. President, you persist in thinking that you can defeat me. You have spent millions of dollars bombing our compound in Kurdistan, and then you were naïve enough to believe that the Iranians would do your bidding. You are all fools to think that you can achieve victory over me. I thought you would have learned the last time, but you don't know when I've beaten you, which I have. The winter that I inflicted on you is only the beginning of my wrath. You will soon wish that you never ran against me for office. Enjoy the weather, Mr. President. You now live in a climate of doubt.

    Yours in conquest,
Bartholomew Martin

CHARACTERS – *A Climate of Doubt*

Abbassi, Ramin – American spy in Iran

Adams, Bill – Mayor of New York City

Arnold, Jake – White House Chief of Staff

Bellamy, Ellen – TV Talk Show Host and Rick's wife

Bellamy, Rick – Secretary of Homeland Security and Ellen's Husband

Boynton, Sally – FBI Agent and Secretary Bellamy's assistant

Buster – CIA Agent

Carlini, William –Director, CIA

Collins, Gregory – Admiral, Chief of Naval Operations

Columbo, Bob – CIA agent and voice impersonator

Cranston, Bill - Astronaut

Crawford, Michael – Aeronautical engineer

Deming, Nigel – English meteorologist

Dolan, Roger – Chairman of the Joint Chiefs of Staff

Drake, Walter – Senior FBI agent at Rosetta Corporation

Duncan, Phil – Operations VP, the Rosetta Corporation

Foreman, Jack – Interim CEO of Rosetta

Hardy, David – *Moonwalker* astronaut

Jackson, Mark – Astronaut for *The Reformers*

Jordan, Michael – *Moonwalker* astronaut

Khamenei, Ali – Supreme Leader of Iran

Langdon, Jerome – Secretary of State

Laub, Jerome - Astronaut for *The Reformers*

Martin, Bartholomew – 46th President of the United States

McCallum, Martha – Reporter for *Fox News*

Merriman, Douglas – Assistant to Bartholomew Martin

Morgan, Frank – CEO Rosetta Corporation

Mullin, Nancy – Astronaut

O'Keefe, Elliott – TV Producer

Patterson, Mike – Colonel, USAF, Commander of *Ranger*

Peterson, Dwight – Climate expert

Rashadi, Hamid – Deputy Foreign Minister of Iran

Roker, Al – Meteorologist and TV personality

Sproule, Jack – Meteorologist

Tomkins, James – Climate expert

Watson, Mike – Novelist and Sarah's husband

Watson, Sarah – Director of the FBI

Whalen, Jack – Major, USAF, Astronaut

A NOTE FROM THE AUTHOR

Thank you for reading *A Climate of Doubt*. I hope you enjoyed reading it as much as I enjoyed writing it.

Please consider writing a brief review on Amazon.com. Reviews are the lifeblood of an author.

Russ Moran

ABOUT THE AUTHOR

Russ Moran is the author of 12 novels. *The Gray Ship*, Book One of *The Time Magnet* series, is a story of time travel, alternate history, romance, and a nuclear warship that finds itself in the Civil War. *The Thanksgiving Gang* is the sequel, *A Time of Fear* is Book Three, *The Skies of Time* is Book Four, and *The Keepers of Time* is Book Five.

The Shadows of Terror is Book One of The Patterns series, followed by *The Scent of Revenge*.

A Reunion in Time is a time travel novel, but not in the Time Magnet series.

Sideswiped, a legal thriller, is Book One of the Matt Blake Series.

The Reformers is Book Two of the Matt Blake Series, and *The President is Missing* is Book Three. Matt Blake, as you just read, is a major character in *A Climate of Doubt*.

Robot Depot, is a novel about our automated future.

Moran also published five nonfiction books: *Justice in America: How it Works—How it Fails; The APT Principle: The Business Plan That You Carry in Your Head; Boating Basics: The Boattalk Book of Boating Tips; If You're Injured: A Consumer Guide to Personal Injury Law; How to Create More Time.* He's a lawyer and a veteran of the United States Navy. He lives on Long Island, New York, with his wife, Lynda and their two dogs, Maggie the Golden Retriever and Sammy the Shitzu.

The Gray Ship – **Book One of** *The Time Magnet Series*

http://amzn.to/16GPumH

"This provocative, intensely powerful novel is a must-read for sci-fi fans and Civil War aficionados, though mainstream fiction readers will find it heart-rending and inspiring as well. A rare read that's not only wildly entertaining, but also profoundly moving." — Kirkus Reviews

The Thanksgiving Gang – **Book Two of** *The Time Magnet Series*

http://amzn.to/1NzBs7N

"I had never read a book before written in an efficient, minimalistic prose... Instead of writing what most readers want to read, he gives voice to life-like characters, with their flaws and prejudices. They are not infallible superheroes. It's always nice to find a new voice in fiction and to enjoy creativity at its best." — C. Ludewig. "Breakneck pacing and virtually nonstop action" – Kirkus Reviews

A Time of Fear – **Book Three of** *The Time Magnet Series*

http://amzn.to/1zdjaG9

"His story is fascinating, and adds even more depth to this already cavernously deep novel. Amazingly unique, chilling and well written, Moran weaves a future that is both desperate and hopeful. Blending modern fears with science fiction results in a tale that will keep you reading long into the night." Five stars!" —Heather

The Skies of Time – **Book Four of** *The Time Magnet Series*

http://amzn.to/1CCC3jg

In *The Skies of Time*, you will recognize the two main characters, Ashley Patterson, now an admiral, and her husband, Jack Thurber. They met and fell in love in *The Gray Ship*, and now they're in for the adventure of their lives in *The Skies of Time*. Ashley and Jack have been such prominent characters in all four books of The Time Magnet Series that I feel like they're old friends. You will also recognize some of the other characters. But if I told you who they are, it would ruin the fun.

"I'm a big fan of this series and this one may be the best. I hope there is another book to this series since it keeps getting better. There are a few questions I have about certain events that makes the next one even more suspenseful. These are great books to binge read one after the other." — Time Travel Fan

The Shadows of Terror – Book One of the *Patterns Series*

http://amzn.to/1IDQzJS

A novel that explodes off the front page of your newspaper.

Terrorism now has a new face, a face that's obscured in the shadows. The radical forces of destruction have learned to make themselves invisible to the West, and preventing a terrorist attack has become almost impossible.

A new war has begun, World War III.

Rick Bellamy, an FBI agent who specializes in counterterrorism, is engaged in his own war, a war with no end.

Bellamy's wife, Ellen, a prominent architect, discovers that she's in the middle of the greatest terror plot to date.

To defeat the enemy, Bellamy first has to uncover the clues, to shine a light on the shadows. He has to find patterns – before it's too late.

"Move over James Patterson and Mary Higgins Clark. There's a new guy in town. Russ Moran's new book – *The Shadows of Terror.*" — Frank from Lynbrook

The Scent of Revenge, - Book Two in the *Patterns Series.*

http://amzn.to/1UvDRmw

The world is at war – World War III. FBI Agent Rick Bellamy and his wife, Ellen, find themselves in the middle of a sinister terror plot.

Someone is attacking young prominent women, inflicting a horrible disease.

Nobody knows its origin, nobody knows how to stop it, nobody knows how to cure it.

Rick Bellamy and a team of scientists want to go on offense. But how?

Will the lives of the women be changed forever? When will the attacks stop?

"Heart pounding, can't put down thriller that will force you to look at terrorism in different light. Life in America will never be the same." —Cold Coffee Cafe

Sideswiped - Book One in the Matt Blake series of legal thrillers.

http://amzn.to/1MkxX35

Trial lawyer Matt Blake took on a perfect case.

It involved a sideswipe collision in which his client's husband, an investigative reporter, was killed. The evidence of negligence was overwhelming. Eyewitnesses testified that defendant was talking on his cell phone when he hit the other car.

But was it negligence? Was it an accident?

Or was it murder?

Matt uncovers evidence that the act may have been intentional. Somebody wanted the man silenced. Somebody wanted the man dead.

Somebody had a lot to hide.

The signs started to point to the highest levels of government.

An open-and-shut personal injury case suddenly became a vast conspiracy of terror.

"This book hooks you in from the first line. *Sideswiped* draws you into the world of Matt Blake and you become emotionally attached to him and his journey. The story itself is so well-written and moves quickly so there is never a dull moment." —Sarah Elle

"Moran demonstrates the depth of his writing talent by developing a new genre with *Sideswiped*, a legal thriller. Branching out from his previous novels dealing with time travel, Moran goes in a whole new direction with Book One in the Matt Blake series. He creates a wild but totally believable story of modern day intrigue and suspense. Moran also deftly weaves into this book some of my favorite characters from his prior novels. I am looking forward to starting Book #2 - *The Reformers* — Frank from Lynbrook on August 16, 2016

The Reformers - Book Two of the Matt Blake series of legal thrillers, is the sequel to *Sideswiped*.

http://amzn.to/2m8uMdu

The forces of radical Islam are on the run.

Their leadership has been decimated, their ranks thinned, their power disappearing by the week.

Their recruiting efforts have been cut off, the radical websites shut down, and the attraction of jihad is losing its appeal among the young.

With targeted assassinations, military strikes, as well as the loss of oil fields and gold mines, radical Islam is fast losing power.

But who is responsible?

It isn't the United States Government. It's a new force the world has never seen before.

Lawyer Matt Blake and his wife Diana find themselves in the middle of the most gigantic plot the world has ever seen, a conspiracy that's only begun to grow.

"I've been a fan of the author, Russell Moran, since reading *Sideswiped* a few months ago, so I admittedly went into this book with quite high expectations. That being said, I had no idea that "*The Reformers*" was going to play out in the way that it does and I can see myself giving this book a re-read in the future. In fact, I am even more impressed by the storyline of this read than the last and it has left me excited to see more." Lucidity.

The Keepers of Time – Book Five of the Time Magnet Series

http://amzn.to/2wjVSTt

Admiral Ashley Patterson and her husband Jack have done it again. They've traveled through time, 200 years into the future—aboard a nuclear aircraft carrier, Ashley's flagship.

They discover a new world, a strange new world—a post-nuclear war world—one that is both a beacon of hope, and a cry of despair.

They meet a group of people who call themselves *The Keepers of Time,* an organization dedicated to preserving history and culture.

But the world around them has harkened back to a primitive and savage past, one that includes human sacrifice.

Ashley knows they have to have to get back to the present to warn the government of the unspeakable horrors that await.

But finding the way back to the present is their greatest challenge, an almost insurmountable one.

"A wild time travel yarn that starts fast and doesn't slow down until the end."

A Reunion in Time

http://amzn.to/2tneIsg

What if a 37-year-old adult travels back 20 years in time and finds himself in high school, followed by his 36-year-old wife? They're now teenagers, 17 and 16.

Adults in teenage bodies, they struggle to convince the people from their past that they are real, not apparitions. With the benefit of hindsight, they know the history of the past 20 years, and it isn't pretty.

Rick and Ellen are married, and now have to adjust to married life as teenagers in 2001. Rick is a senior FBI official and Ellen is a famous architect.

But everybody sees them as kids. Nobody believes that they're married, and nobody believes their stories—until Rick and Ellen predict 9/11.

How do they find their way back to the year they came from? How do they warn the authorities of the cataclysm that will occur in the future? The answer is to find the time portal—the wormhole—that brought them to 2001. But the site has changed. It's no longer the place where they crossed the wormhole. Will they live out the balance of their lives beginning as teenagers? "We've all wish we could go back to earlier times with the mind we have now. This Russell Moran book takes you there and it is a fun creative Romp well worth reading. *A Reunion in Time* is highly recommend!" Kindle Customer.

The President is Missing – Book Three of the Matt Blake series.

http://amzn.to/2t9v7wu

While he was addressing the nation from a submerged nuclear submarine, President Blake's message is suddenly cut off. Anyone listening heard an explosion. The explosion was followed by floating debris five minutes later.

First Lady Dee Blake has doubts, which she shares with naval high command and the new president. She thinks the explosion and the debris were a ruse to make people think the sub was destroyed, and her husband with it.

Could the sub have been hijacked and the president kidnapped?

But who would commit such an act? What is its purpose?

Was it Russia, China, Iran, or a shadowy group of freelance terrorists?

The new president appoints Dee as his Chief of Staff, with explicit instructions to find the missing submarine—and President Matt Blake.

Her life, and the life of the nation, suddenly take a horrifying turn.

Robot Depot

https://amzn.to/2pWIIqy

Robot Depot is a book about our automated present - and future.

Mike Bateman is a visionary businessman, the creator, and CEO of the fabulously successful chain of stores, Robot Depot, a company dedicated to selling robots and Artificial Intelligence machines for a variety of uses.

One of Robot Depot's engineers invented the world's first sentient robot, one that is aware of its own existence. That robot's name is Angus, named after a famous inventor. Angus invents an algorithm that revolutionizes medical science, a program that accurately diagnoses an illness and recommends a treatment, within 15 seconds.

Whether it's a floor cleaner, a window washer, an intelligent drone, or a medical diagnosis algorithm, Robot Depot has a device for you.

The company is a darling of Wall Street and is the most popular destination for consumers and businesses looking for labor saving devices.

But the company has caught the eye of ISIS, the terrorist Islamic State. They discover a great way to deliver bombs – using the products of Robot Depot to kill people.

Within a matter of days, a skyscraper is destroyed, houses are burned to the ground, a cruise ship is disabled, Yankee Stadium is attacked, and a children's sailing regatta is bombed.

Overnight, Robot Depot changed from being a popular company to an object of fear because of the tampered products it sells.

Mike Bateman and his wife Jenny discover the true horror of terrorism one frightening summer morning.

"I highly recommend this book to anyone who enjoys crisp writing, thought-provoking topics, and colorful characters. Well-done Mr. Moran." Amazon verified review